"I told dad he should marry you," Toby said

"Toby, you didn't!" Eve nearly dropped the dish in her hand, a warm pink flooding her cheeks.

"Yes, I did," he assured her innocently. "What's wrong with that? He likes you—I know he does. I saw him kiss you."

Eve became very busy with the dishes. "Just because you kiss someone doesn't necessarily mean you want to marry them, Toby."

"Yeah, that's what dad said," he admitted. "But we need someone around here to take care of us. Somewhere there's a girl that dad will marry. I just gotta find her."

"Toby McClure, I think you should leave that to your father," Eve warned.

"Yeah, but he isn't *trying* to find anybody," Toby protested. "I thought I'd have better luck."

JANET DAILEY AMERICANA

M

Janet Dailey
Americana

WITH A
LITTLE LUCK

Harlequin Books

TORONTO • NEW YORK • LONDON
AMSTERDAM • PARIS • SYDNEY • HAMBURG
STOCKHOLM • ATHENS • TOKYO • MILAN

The state flower depicted on the cover of this book is
wood violet.

Janet Dailey Americana edition published June 1988
Second printing November 1988
Third printing November 1989

ISBN 373-21949-0

Harlequin Presents edition published February 1982

Original hardcover edition published in 1981
by Mills & Boon Limited

CHAPTER ONE

"ARE YOU SURE you wouldn't like a ride home?" the Reverend Mr. Johnson inquired. "If you don't mind waiting a few minutes, I would be happy to drive you."

Mr. Johnson didn't look like a minister in his plaid shirt and khaki-colored pants. In his midforties, he resembled a fisherman who had strayed into church by mistake. In fact, he was an ardent angler, overjoyed that his Wisconsin parish was situated in an area with so many lakes, streams and rivers. He loved to state that while he was a "fisher of men" like the Lord, he was also a fisherman, an occupation and an avocation that he felt were ideally suited to one another.

"No, thank you, Reverend. It's a lovely evening and I'll enjoy the walk," Eve Rowland insisted as she slipped on her summer-weight coat of brown. "Besides, it isn't that far, really."

"Yes, but I don't like the idea of your walking alone after dark."

"Cable isn't Minneapolis or Milwaukee," she laughed. There were times when she even forgot to lock the front door of her parents' house, but she didn't worry unduly on those occasions.

"My city background is showing, isn't it?" he smiled at himself. "Thanks for filling in for Mrs. Alstrom at the organ tonight." She was the regular church organist. A minor crisis at home had kept her from attending choir practice and Eve had been asked to substitute for her. "I hope it didn't upset any of your plans for the evening."

"I didn't have any plans," she said, and didn't go any further in her reply. It was rare for her ever to have plans for an evening—social plans, that is.

"That's a pity." The minister's eyes darkened with sympathy, even as he changed his expression to give her an encouraging smile. "You are a warm and generous woman. Maybe I should whisper in the ears of the eligible male members of my congregation."

He meant to be kind but his offer had a demoralizing effect. Eve fixed a quick smile in place to hide her reaction. "That's a nice thought, but most of them are already semiattached to someone else. You might as well save your matchmaking talents for another time." She started to leave. "Good night. And I'm glad I could help out."

"I'll see you in church on Sunday." Mr. Johnson lifted his hand in a saluting wave.

"Not this Sunday," she said. "We're opening

the summer cottage on the lake, so neither my parents nor I will be in church."

"Oh? Which lake?" His fishing curiosity was awakened.

"Namekagon." Which was only a few miles east of town.

"Marvelous fishing there," he stated.

"I know. It's dad's favorite." She glanced at her wristwatch, a utilitarian piece with a plain leather band that made no pretense of being decorative. "I'd better be going. Good night, Reverend Johnson."

"Good night."

Leaving the church, Eve buttoned her coat against the invading night air. Although it was officially summer, the temperature in the Northwoods dipped to the cool range in the evening hours. The sky was crystal bright with stars, hundreds of thousands of them lighting the heavens. A moon, big and fat, competed with the stars; its silver globe was nearly a spotlight shining down on the earth. The streetlights along the main thoroughfare were almost unneeded.

As she walked along the sidewalk, her mind kept echoing the matchmaking offer the minister had made. Having lived in Cable for all of her twenty-six years—with the exception of four years spent at college in Madison—Eve knew virtually every single man in the area. Those she might have been interested in never noticed her;

and those that noticed her she wasn't interested in. She was almost convinced she was too particular.

Her mother despaired that Eve would ever find a man who could satisfy her, and kept reminding her that with each passing year she was becoming more set in her ways. Eve had given up hope long ago that Prince Charming would ever come this far north, but she wasn't going to get married just for the sake of being married, no matter how nice and respectable a suitor might be. She didn't intend to marry unless she had, at least, a deep affection for the man. So far, no one had aroused even that. There had been boyfriends now and then. Most of them she genuinely liked, but not with any depth. It seemed she was always attracted to men who weren't attracted to her.

It wasn't because she was homely. She was attractive, in a plain sort of way. With brown hair and eyes, she had a flawless complexion, but her features were unassuming. Her figure was average, neither thin nor plump. She wasn't too tall or too short. She simply didn't stand out in a crowd. In a sea of pretty faces, hers would be the last to be noticed.

Eve was just as realistic in her assessment of her personality traits. She was intelligent, basically good-natured and possessed a good sense of humor. As a music teacher, she appreciated music and the arts. But she tended to be quiet and not quick to make friends. Her early years as a wallflower had lessened her inclination for parties. She preferred celebrating with a few close friends to attending a large social function. By nature she wasn't aggressive, although she wouldn't allow herself to be walked on.

There were some who suggested that, at twenty-six, she was too old to be living at home. When Eve considered the cost of living alone versus her salary, it became a matter of sheer practicality. Besides, she and her parents were good friends. She was just as independent as she would have been living in an apartment.

With all her thoughts focused inward, Eve didn't notice the tavern she was approaching. A window was open to let out the smoke and let in fresh air. Inside, a jukebox was loudly playing a popular song. Eve didn't hear it or the laughter and spirited voices. Her gaze was on the sidewalk in front of her feet.

Suddenly a man stepped directly in front of her. Eve didn't have time to stop or step aside. Her hands came up to absorb the shock of the collision. He evidently didn't see her, either, as he took a step forward and collided head-on. In a reflex action his arms went around to catch her, while his forward progress carried her backward two steps.

Dazed by the total unexpectedness of the accident, Eve lifted her head. She wasn't certain that the fault belonged entirely to either one of them. Too stunned yet to speak, she stared at the stranger she'd bumped into—or vice versa.

The light from the neon tavern sign fully illuminated his face. Nearly a head taller than she was, he had dark hair that waved in thick strands to fall at a rakish angle across his forehead. His eyes were blue, with a perpetual glint of humor in them. Tanned skin was stretched across very masculine features. He was handsome in a tough rakehell sort of way. A reckless smile showed the white of his teeth.

"What's this I've caught?" His mocking voice was matched by the laughing glint in his eyes as they traveled over her, taking in the brown of her hair and eyes and the brown coat. "I believe it's a brown mouse."

The teasing remark did not go down well, considering the earlier demoralizing remark by the minister. Her gaze dropped to the cream-colored pullover and the thin-striped blue-and-cream color of his shirt collar. Since he had obviously just left the tavern, Eve wasn't surprised that there was liquor on his breath. He'd been drinking, but he wasn't drunk. He was steady on his feet, and there was no glaze of alcohol in the rich blue of his eyes.

"I'm sorry," Eve apologized stiffly. "I wasn't paying attention to where I was going." Then she realized his arms were still holding her and her hands were flattened against his chest—a very solid chest. Her heart began to beat unevenly.

"I wasn't looking where *I* was going, so it seems we were both to blame, brown mouse. Did I hurt you?" It was more disturbing to listen to the low pitch of his voice without seeing his face, so Eve looked up. His half-closed eyes were difficult to meet squarely.

"No, you didn't." When he showed no inclination to release her, she stated, "I'm all right. You can let go of me now."

"Must I?" he sighed deeply. His hands moved, but not away from her. Instead they began roaming over her shoulders and spine in an exploring fashion, as if testing the way she felt in his arms. "Do you know how long it's been since I held a woman in my arms?"

The well-shaped line of his mouth held a latent sensuality as his question confirmed the direction that Eve had suspected his thoughts were taking. His hands were exerting a slight pressure to inch her closer to him. They were standing on the sidewalk of a main street a few feet away from a tavern full of people.

Surely he wouldn't try to accost her in such a place? She wanted to struggle, but she was afraid he might view it as provocation rather than resistance. Yet she recognized the inherent danger in the situation. She kept her body rigid.

"Would you please let me go?" she requested.

"I'm frightening you, aren't I?" He tipped his head to one side, regarding her lazily, while his hands stopped their movement.

"Yes," Eve admitted, because her heart was beating a mile a minute and there was a choked sensation in her throat.

He let his hands slide away to let her stand free. She had expected an argument. It was a full second before she realized he was no longer holding her. She brushed past him and was a step beyond him when his hand snaked out to catch her arm.

"Don't scurry off into the dark, brown mouse." His voice chided her for running. "Stay a minute."

"No." His hand forced her to stop, but she lifted her arm in protest of his grip, straining against the unyielding strength of his fingers.

"What's your hurry? Are you meeting someone?"

The questions were curious, interested.

"No." Eve was confused and wary. He wouldn't release her, but he was making no move to do more than keep her there.

"Where are you going in such a rush?" Shadows fell across his face to throw the angles and planes of his features into harsh relief. They enhanced his rough virility, adding to the aura of dangerous attraction.

"I'm going home," she stated.

"I don't have any place to go but home, either," he said. "So why don't we go some place together? Then we won't have to go home."

"I want to go home," Eve insisted firmly, despite the faint quiver that was spreading up her arm from the restraining touch of his hand.

"Why? It's lonely there."

She had difficulty imagining a man like him ever being lonely. It was obviously a line. She wasn't going to be strung along by it.

"Let me put it another way: I don't want to go with you."

"I think I'm giving you the wrong impression." A half smile slanted his mouth, casually disarming. "I want to go someplace where we can talk."

Another line, Eve guessed. "I doubt that you're interested in talking," she returned with a tinge of sarcasm.

"It's true," he insisted, and moved to stand more to the front of her, without letting go of her arm.

Eve stared straight ahead in an effort to ignore him and the strange leaping of her pulse. His other hand moved to touch the side of her silky brown hair. Instinctively she jerked away from the soft caress, preferring force to his present means of intimidating her. She turned her head to stare at him.

When she met his gaze, Eve realized he was a man who communicated by touching—with his hands or his gaze. . .or his mouth and his body. Unbidden, her mind had added the last. She didn't doubt his expertise in any area. Her composure began to splinter a little, undermined by her unexpectedly wayward imagination.

"It is true," he repeated. "Don't you know that a man can talk to a brown mouse?"

Which was hardly flattering in the light of her own low opinion of her sex appeal.

"Would you please not call me that?" Irritation flashed through her as she refused to comment on his observation.

"I always wondered if a brown mouse would retaliate when it was backed into a corner. There is some spirit there, behind that apparent timidity." It was obvious by the look of satisfaction on his face that she had heightened his interest. Eve wished she had kept her mouth shut. "A brown mouse. That's what you are, you know. With your brown hair and your brown eyes and your brown coat."

He was baiting her, but this time she ignored him. "I am a brown mouse who is anxious to go home, so would you let me go?" She injected a weary note in her voice, as if she were finding him quite tiresome. Fleetingly it occurred to her that she wouldn't be in this situation if she had accepted the Reverend Mr. Johnson's offer of a ride home.

"If you insist that's what you want to do, I'll walk with you to make sure you arrive safely and no cat pounces on you on the way home."

"I can think of only one 'cat' that might pounce on me and that's you," Eve retorted.

"Touché!" he laughed, and she was upset with herself for liking the sound of it.

She faced him directly. "If you don't leave me alone, I'm going to have to scream."

"Mice squeak," he corrected, but his gaze had narrowed on her, judging to see how serious she was about her threat.

"This brown mouse screams," she insisted.

She could, and if she felt sufficiently threatened, she would. It hadn't reached that point yet, but this conversation had gone on long enough.

"I believe she does," he agreed after a second had passed. He released her arm and lifted his hands in a mocking indication that he wouldn't touch her again.

"Thank you." Eve wasn't sure why she said that. Immediately she began walking away, trying not to walk too fast. She could feel him watching her with those magnetic blue eyes. It was an unnerving sensation.

"Good night, brown mouse." His low voice called after her, a hint of regret in its tone.

She didn't answer him. For another ten feet, Eve wondered if he would start following her. She forced herself not to look back. A few seconds later she heard the tavern door open and close. She glanced over her shoulder, but he wasn't in sight. Since no customer had come out, he had obviously gone back inside. She didn't have to wonder anymore whether he would come after her. Instead Eve found herself wondering who he was.

It was after ten when she reached her home. Both her parents were in the living room when she walked in. Neither of them was particularly striking in his appearance. Her father was a tall spare man with hazel eyes and thinning brown hair, while her mother was petitely built, with graying brown hair and brown eyes. It was a toss-up from whom Eve had inherited her common looks.

"Choir practice must have run late," her mother observed. It was a statement of conversation, not a remark about Eve's lateness in getting home.

"A little." She shrugged out of her brown coat and wondered if she would ever wear it again without thinking of herself as a brown mouse. "Mr. Johnson offered me a ride home, but it was such a lovely evening I decided to walk. So it took a little longer."

She didn't mention the stranger outside the tavern. They were still her parents. Eve didn't want to cause them needless concern. It had been a harmless incident anyway, not worth recounting.

IN THE MIDDLE OF THE NIGHT Toby McClure rolled onto his side. His long, little boy lashes fluttered, his sleep disturbed by a faint sound. He slowly let them come open, his sleepy blue eyes focusing on the door to his bedroom, which stood ajar. Listening, he heard hushed movement in another part of the house. A smile touched the corners of his mouth and deepened when he heard the person bump into a chair and curse beneath his breath.

Throwing back the covers, Toby slipped out of his single bed and walked to the hall door. His bare feet made no sound on the carpeted floor. He opened the door wide and waited until he saw the towering frame of his father separate from the darkness. He was walking unsteadily, trying so hard to be quiet.

The light from the full moon streamed through the window at the end of the hallway where Toby stood, including him in its path. The instant he saw the boy, his father, Luck McClure, stopped abruptly and swayed, bracing a hand against the wall to steady himself. A frown gathered on his forehead as he eyed the boy.

"What are you doing out of bed? You're supposed to be asleep," he accused in a growling voice that had a trace of a slur.

"You woke me up," Toby replied. "You always do when you try to sneak in."

"I wasn't sneaking." He emphatically denied that suggestion and glanced around. "Where's Mrs. Jackson, the lady who is supposed to be sitting with you?"

"She was going to charge double after midnight, so I paid her off and sent her home. You owe me twelve dollars.''

"You—" Luck McClure clamped his mouth shut on the explosion of anger and carefully raised a hand to cradle his forehead. "We'll talk about this in the morning, Toby," he declared in heavy warning.

"Yes, sir. I'll remind you if you forget," he promised. A mischievous light danced in his eyes. "You owe me twelve dollars.''

"That's another thing we'll discuss in the morning." But it was a weak facsimile of his previous warning, as a wave of tiredness washed over him. "Right now, I'm going to bed."

Luck pushed away from the wall and used that impetus to carry him to the bedroom door opposite his son's. Toby watched him open the door to the darkened room and head in the general direction of the bed. Without a light to see the exact location of his destination, Luck stubbed his toe on an end post. He started to swear and stopped sharply when Toby crossed the hall to flip the switch, turning on the overhead light.

"Why aren't you back in bed where you belong?" Luck hobbled around to the side of the bed and half sat, half fell onto the mattress.

"I figured you'd need help getting ready for bed." Toby walked to the bed with all the weary patience of an adult and helped finish tugging the pullover sweater over his father's head.

"For an eight-year-old kid, you figure a lot of things," Luck observed with a wry sort of affection. While he unbuttoned the cuffs of his shirt, Toby unfastened the buttons on his shirtfront.

"You've gotta admit, dad, I did you a favor tonight," Toby said as he helped pull his arms free of the shirt. "How would it have looked if Mrs. Jackson had seen you come home drunk?"

"I'm not drunk," Luck protested, unfastening his pants and standing long enough to slip them down his hips. Toby pulled them the rest of the way off. "I just had a few drinks, that's all."

"Sure, dad." He reached over and pulled down the bedcovers. It didn't take much persuasion to get his father under them.

"It feels so good to lie down," Luck groaned, and started to shut his eyes when Toby tucked the covers around him. He opened them to give his son a bleary-eyed look. "Did I tell you I talked to a brown mouse?" The question was barely out before he rolled onto his side, burrowing into the pillow. "You'd better get some sleep, son," he mumbled.

Shaking his head, Toby walked to the door and paused to look at his already snoring father. He reached up to flip off the light.

"A brown mouse," he repeated. "That's another thing we'll discuss in the morning."

Back in his moonlit room, Toby crawled into bed. He glanced at the framed photograph on

the table beside his bed. The picture was a twin
to the one on his father's bureau. From it, a
tawny-haired blonde with green eyes smiled
back at him—his mother, and easily the most
beautiful woman Toby had ever seen. Not that
he remembered her. He had been a baby when
she died—six years ago today. His gaze strayed
in the direction of his father's bedroom. Sigh-
ing, he closed his eyes.

SHORTLY AFTER EIGHT the next morning, Toby
woke up. He lay there for several minutes before
he finally yawned and climbed out of bed to
stretch. Twenty minutes later he had brushed his
teeth and washed, combed his hair and found a
clean pair of jeans and a yellow T-shirt to wear.

Leaving his bedroom, he paused in the hallway to look in on his father. Luck McClure was
sprawled across the bed, the spare pillow
clutched by an encircling arm. Toby quietly
closed the door, although he doubted his father
would be disturbed by any noise he made.

In the kitchen, he put a fresh pot of coffee on
to perk, then pushed the step stool to the counter and climbed it to reach the juice glasses and a
cereal bowl in the cupboard. Positioning the
stool in front of another cupboard, he mounted
it to take down a box of cornflakes. With
orange juice and milk from the refrigerator,
Toby sat down to the kitchen table to eat his
breakfast of cereal and orange juice.

By the time he'd finished, the coffee was done. He glanced from it to the pitcher of orange juice, hesitated, and walked to the refrigerator to take out a pitcher of tomato juice. Climbing back up the step stool, he took down a tall glass and filled it three-quarters full with tomato juice. When he returned the pitcher to the refrigerator, he took out an egg, cracked it, and added it to the tomato juice. He stirred that mixture hard, then added garlic and Tabasco to it. Sniffing the end result, he wrinkled his nose in distaste.

Taking the glass, he left the kitchen and walked down the hallway to his father's room. He hadn't changed position in bed. Toby leaned over, taking great care not to spill the contents of the glass, and shook his father's shoulder with his free hand.

"It's nine o'clock, dad. Time to get up." His statement drew a groan of protest. "Come on, dad."

With great reluctance, Luck rolled onto his back, flinging an arm across his eyes to shield them from the brightness of the sunlight shining in his window. Toby waited in patient silence until he sat up.

"Oh, my head," Luck mumbled, and held it in both his hands, the bedcovers falling around his waist to leave his torso bare.

Toby climbed onto the bed, balancing on his knees while he offered his father the concoction he'd made. "Drink this. It'll make you feel better."

Lowering his hands part way from his head, Luck looked at it skeptically. "What is it?"

"Don't ask," Toby advised, and reached out to pinch his father's nose closed while he tipped the glass to his lips. He managed to pour a mouthful down before his father choked and took the glass out of his hand.

"What is this?" Luck coughed and frowned as he studied the glass.

"It's a hangover remedy." And Toby became the recipient of the glowering frown and a raised eyebrow.

"And when did you become an expert on hangover remedies?" Luck challenged.

"I saw it on television once," Toby shrugged.

Luck shook his head in quiet exasperation. "I should make you drink this, you know that, don't you?" he sighed.

"There's fresh coffee in the kitchen." Toby hopped off the bed, just in case his father intended to carry out that threat.

"Go pour me a cup. And take this with you." A smile curved slowly, forming attractive grooves on either side of his mouth—male dimples—as he handed the glass back to Toby. "I'll be there as soon as I get some clothes on."

"I'll pour you some orange juice, too," Toby volunteered.

"Just straight orange juice. Don't put anything else in it."

"I won't." A wide grin split Toby's face before he turned to walk swiftly from the room.

With a wry shake of his head, Luck threw back the covers and climbed slowly out of bed. He paused beside the bureau to glance at the photograph. *Well, pretty lady, do you see what kind of boy your son has grown into?* The blue of his eyes had a pensive look as he walked to the bathroom.

CHAPTER TWO

"YOUR COFFEE IS COLD," Toby accused when his father finally appeared in the kitchen.

Dressed in worn blue jeans and a gray sweat shirt, Luck had taken the time to shower and shave. His dark brown hair gleamed almost black, combed into a careless kind of order. He smiled at the reproval from his son.

"I had to get cleaned up," he defended himself, and sipped at the lukewarm coffee before adding some hot liquid from the coffeepot. He sat down in a chair opposite from his son and rested his forearms on the table. "Do you want to explain to me what happened to Mrs. Jackson last night?"

"She was going to charge you double for staying after midnight, so I paid her and sent her home," Toby said, repeating his previous night's explanation.

"And she went—just like that," Luck replied with a wave of his hand to indicate how easy it had been. "She just went and left you here alone?"

"Well. . ." Toby hedged, and squirmed in his chair.

"Why did she leave?"

"She got the impression we were broke, I think. She got a little upset thinking that you'd asked her to stay when you knew all you could afford to pay was twelve dollars."

"Why did you do it?"

"I'm too old to have a sitter, dad," Toby protested. "I can take care of myself."

"Maybe you can, but what about my peace of mind? I'm an adult. You're a child. When I leave, I want to know there's an adult with you—looking after you—yes. But mostly in case there's an emergency—if you should get sick or hurt. I'd like to know there is someone here with you to help," he explained firmly. "Do you understand?"

"Yes." It was a low admission.

"From now on, when I go out for the evening, you will have a sitter and she will stay here until I come back. Is that understood?"

"Yes."

"Good." With the discussion concluded, Luck raised the coffee cup to his mouth.

"What about the twelve dollars?" As far as Toby was concerned, the discussion wasn't over. "It's from the money I've been saving to buy a minibike."

"You should have considered that before you spent it."

"But that's what you would have had to pay her if I hadn't," Toby reasoned with the utmost logic. "You would have had to pay her that and more."

"I'll give you the twelve dollars back on one condition," Luck replied. "You call Mrs. Jackson, tell her what you did, and apologize."

There was a long sigh before Toby nodded his agreement. "Okay."

"Have you had breakfast?" Luck changed the subject.

"Cornflakes."

"Would you like some bacon and eggs?"

"Sure," Toby agreed. "I'll help."

While he set the table, Luck put the bacon in the skillet and broke eggs in a bowl to scramble them. Finished with his task before his father, Toby walked over to the stove to watch.

"Dad?" He tipped his head back to look up to his tall parent. "Do you want to explain about the brown mouse?"

"The brown mouse?" Luck frowned at him, his expression blank.

"Yeah. Last night when you came home, you said you had talked to a brown mouse," Toby explained. "I thought people only saw pink elephants when they were drinking."

"People can have all kinds of illusions when they are drinking. Evidently mine was a brown mouse," Luck murmured. "I must have had a few more drinks than I realized."

"It was because of mom, wasn't it?" Toby asked quietly.

There was a moment of silence. Then Luck gave him a smiling glance. "What do you want to do today? Do you want to go fishing? Boating? Just name it." He deliberately avoided his son's question, and Toby knew there was no need to repeat it.

"Let's go fishing," Toby decided.

"Fishing it is," Luck agreed, and smiled as he rumpled the top of his son's brown hair.

Two hours later the dishes were washed and the beds were made and they were sitting in the boat, anchored in a cove of Lake Namekagon. A thick forest crowded the meandering shoreline, occasionally leaving room for a sandy stretch of beach. A mixture of hardwood and conifers, with extensive stands of pine and spruce, provided a blend of the green shades of summer. The unruffled calm of the lake reflected the edging wall of forest, home for the black bear, deer, beaver and other wildlife.

Their fishing lines were in the water, their rods resting against the sides of the boat in their stands. Toby was leaning back in his seat, his little-boy legs stretched out in front of him and his hands clasped behind his head for a pillow. He stared at the puffy cloud formations in the blue sky with a frown of concentration.

Luck was equally relaxed, yet suspicious of

the long silence that was only broken by the infrequent lapping of water against the boat or the cry of a bird. His sidelong glance studied the intent expression of his son.

"You seem to be doing some pretty heavy thinking, Toby," he observed, and let his gaze slide skyward when his son glanced at him. "What's on your mind?"

"I've been trying to figure something out." Toby turned his head in the pillow of his hands. The frowning concentration remained fixed in his expression. "What exactly does a mother do?"

The question widened Luck's eyes slightly. The question caused him to recognize that his son had never been exposed to the life of a family unit—father, mother and children. There was only one grandparent living, and no aunts or uncles. During the school year, the weekends were the times they had to share together. Luck had often permitted his son to invite a friend over, sometimes to stay overnight, but mostly to accompany them on an afternoon outing; but Toby had never stayed overnight with any of his friends.

The question was a general one—and a serious one. He couldn't avoid answering it. "Mothers do all sorts of things. They cook, wash dishes, clean the house, take care of you when you're sick, do the laundry, all sorts of things like that. Sometimes they work at a job during the day, too. Mothers remember birthdays without being reminded, make special treats for no reason, and think up games to play when you're bored." He knew it was an inadequate answer because he'd left out the love and the caring that he didn't know how to describe.

When Luck finished, he glanced at his son. Toby was staring at the sky, the frown of concentration replaced with a thoughtful look. "I think we need a mother," he announced after several seconds.

"Why?" The statement touched off a defensive mechanism that made Luck challenge it. "Since when have you and I not been able to manage on our own? I thought we had a pretty good system worked out."

"We do, dad," Toby assured him, then sighed. "I'm just tired of always having to wash dishes and make my bed."

The edges of his mouth deepened in a lazy smile. "Having a mother wouldn't mean you'd get out of doing your share of the daily chores."

Unclasping his hands from behind his head, Toby sat upright. "How do you go about finding a mother?"

"That's my problem." Luck made that point very clear. "In order for you to have a mother, I would have to get married again."

"Do you think you'd *like* to get married again?"

"Don't you think your questions are getting a

little bit personal?'' *And a little bit awkward to handle,* Luck thought as he sat up, a tiny crease running across his forehead.

"I'm your son. If you can't talk to me about it, who can you?" Toby reasoned.

"You are much too old for your age." His blue eyes glinted with dry humor when he met the earnest gaze of his son.

"If you got married again, you could have more children," Toby pointed out. "Have you thought about that?"

"Yes, and I don't know if I could handle another one of you," Luck teased.

With a sigh of exasperation, Toby protested. "Dad, will you please be serious? I am trying to discuss this intelligently with you. You wouldn't necessarily have another boy. You could have a little girl."

"Is that what this is about? Do you want brothers and sisters?" There was something at the bottom of all this interest in a mother. Sooner or later, Luck felt he would uncover the reason.

"Do you know that it's really impossible to have a father-son conversation with you?" Toby declared with adult irritation. "You never answer my questions. You just ask me another. How am I ever going to learn anything?"

"All right." Luck crossed his arms in front of him and adopted a serious look. "What do you want to know?"

"If you met the right girl, would you get married again?"

"Yes, if I met the right girl," he conceded with a slow nod.

With a satisfied smile, Toby resumed his former position stretched out in the seat, his head pillowed in his hands, and stared at the sky. "I'll help you look."

Luck took a deep breath, started to say something, then decided it was wiser to let the subject drop.

THE LAKE COTTAGE was built of logs, complete with a front porch that overlooked the lake across the road. The rustic, yet modern structure was tucked in a forest clearing, a dense stand of pines forming a semicircle around it.

Over the weekend, Eve Rowland and her parents had moved in lock, stock and barrel for the summer. It had been a labor of fun opening up their vacation home again and reawakening happy memories of previous summers.

Standing on the porch, Eve gazed at the azure waters of Namekagon Lake. Here in the northwoods of Wisconsin and Minnesota was where the legend of Paul Bunyan and his blue ox, Babe, was born. According to the tales, Paul and Babe stomped around a little in Namekagon, just one of the many lakes in Wisconsin. Eve could remember looking at a map of the area as a child and believing the tale. The mythical figure of Paul Bunyan had been as real to her as the Easter Bunny and Santa Claus, even if he didn't pass out presents.

Eve lifted her head to the clear blue sky and breathed in the clean pine-scented air. On a sigh of contentment, Eve turned and walked into the cottage. It was small, just two bedrooms, the kitchen separated from the living room by a table nook. She let the screen door bang shut. Her father had his fishing gear spread over the table and was working on one of his reels. Her mother was in the kitchen, fixing some potato salad to chill for the evening meal.

"Is it all right if I use the car?" Eve asked. "I want to go to the store down the road. I'm out of shampoo and I'm going to need some suntan lotion."

"Sure." Her father reached in his pants' pocket and tossed her the car keys.

"Was there anything you needed?" Eve reached to pick up her canvas purse where she'd left it on a sofa cushion.

"Maybe some milk," her mother answered, "but other than that, I can't think of anything."

"Okay. I'll be back later," she called over her shoulder as she pushed open the door to the porch.

Sliding into the driver's seat of the sedan, Eve felt as bright and sunny as the summer afternoon. She had dressed to match her mood that day. The terry-cloth material of her short-sleeved top and slacks was a cheerful canary yellow, trimmed with white. A white hairband kept her brown hair away from her face, framing its oval shape.

It was a short drive to the combination grocery and general store that served the resort community. The Rowland family had traded there many times in past summers, so Eve was a familiar face to the owners. She chatted with them a few minutes as she paid for her purchases.

When she started to leave, she heard a man's voice ask to speak to the owner. It sounded vaguely familar, but when she turned to see if it was anyone she knew, the man was hidden from her view by an aisle. Since the man had business with the owner, and since it was possible she didn't even know him, Eve continued out of the store, dismissing the incident from her mind.

She'd left the car in the store's parking area. She walked toward it, but it was only when she got closer that she began to realize something was wrong. Her steps slowed and her eyes widened in disbelief at the sight of the shattered windshield and the three-inch-diameter hole in the glass.

Stunned, Eve absently glanced in the side window and saw the baseball lying on the front seat. Reacting mechanically, she opened the door and reached to pick up the ball amid the splintered chips of glass on the car seat.

"That's my ball." A young boy's voice claimed ownership of the object in her hand.

Still too stunned to be angry or upset, Eve turned to look at him. A baseball cap was perched atop a mass of dark brown hair, while a pair of unblinking innocent blue eyes stared back at her. Eve judged the boy to be eight, no older than nine. She had the feeling that she had seen him somewhere before, possibly at school.

"Did you do this?" She gestured toward the broken windshield, using the same hand that held the baseball.

"Not exactly. You see, my dad just bought me this new baseball glove." He glanced at the oversized leather mitt on his left hand. "We were trying it out to see how it worked. I asked dad to throw me a hard one so I could tell whether there was enough padding to keep my hand from stinging. Only when he did, it was too high and the ball hit the tip of my glove and bounced off, then smashed your windshield. It must have hit it just right," he declared with a rueful grimace. "So it was really my dad who threw the ball. I just didn't catch it."

"A parking lot isn't the place to play catch." At the moment, that was the only thing Eve could think of to say. It was a helpless kind of protest, lacking the strength to change a deed that was already done.

"We know that now," the boy agreed.

"Where's your father?"

"He went into the store to see if they knew who the car belonged to," he explained. "He told me to stay here in case you came back while he was gone."

The comment jogged her memory of the man who had been in the store asking to speak to the owner. She started to turn when she heard the same voice ask, "Is this your car?"

"It's my father's." Eve completed the turn to face the boy's father.

Cold shock froze her limbs into immobility. It was the stranger she'd met outside the tavern last week. The rumpled darkness of his hair grew in thick waves, a few strands straying onto his forehead. The same magnetic blue eyes were looking at her with warm interest. The sunlight added a rough vitality to the handsomely masculine features.

Eve waited, unconsciously holding her breath, for the recognition to show in his eyes as she mentally braced herself to watch that mouth with its ready smile form the words "brown mouse." But it didn't happen. He didn't recognize her. Evidently the combination of liquor and the night's shadows had made her image hazy in his mind. Eve just hoped it stayed that way, as feeling began to steal back into her limbs.

He glanced at the baseball in her hand. "I hope Toby explained what happened." His expression was pleasant, yet serious.

"Yes, he did." She was conscious of how loudly her heart was pounding. "At least he said you threw the ball and he missed it."

"I'm afraid that's what happened," he admitted with a faintly rueful lift of his mouth. "Naturally I'll pay the cost of having the windshield replaced on your father's car, Miss—"

"Rowland. Eve Rowland." She introduced herself and was glad that between the sack of groceries in one arm and the ball in the other hand, she wasn't able to shake hands.

"My name is Luck McClure, and this is my son, Toby." He laid a hand on the boy's shoulder with a trace of parental pride. "We're spending the summer at a lake house a few miles from here."

Eve was certain she had misunderstood his name. "Did you say Luke McClure?"

"No." He smiled, as if it were a common mistake. "It's Luck—as in good luck. Although in actual fact the proper name of Luck has its derivations in the name of Luke or Lucias. It's one of those family names that somehow manages to get passed along to future generations."

"I see," she murmured, and glanced at Toby, who had obviously not been named after his father. She wondered if there were another little Luck somewhere at home. At least now she understood why the boy had seemed familiar at first. There was a definite resemblance between him and his father.

"With that windshield smashed, you aren't going to be able to see to drive home," Luck stated. "I would appreciate it if you would let us give you a ride."

Under the circumstances, Eve didn't know any other way that she could get back to the cottage if she didn't accept his offer. "Yes, thank you," she nodded.

"May I have my baseball back?" the boy spoke up.

"Of course." She handed it to him.

"Our car is parked over here." Luck McClure reclaimed her attention, directing her toward a late-model Jaguar. "Did you say the car was your father's?"

"Yes. He's at the cottage."

"Is that where you would like me to drive you?" He walked around to open the passenger door for her, while his son climbed in the back seat.

"Yes. My parents and I are spending the summer there." Eve waited until he was behind the wheel to give him directions.

"That isn't far from our house," he commented, and Eve wished it was in the opposite direction. Any minute now she just knew he was going to recognize her, which would make things uncomfortable, if not embarrassing. "I'll make arrangements with your father about paying for the windshield."

Briefly Eve wondered if that was a slur at her

sex, insinuating that she wasn't capable of making adequate arrangements because she was a woman. She doubted it, though. Luck McClure was definitely all man, but he didn't strike her as the chauvinistic type. More than likely he simply wanted to deal directly with the owner of the car. Which suited her fine. The less she saw of him, the less chance there would be that he'd remember her.

The rounded bill of a baseball cap entered her side vision as the boy leaned over the seat. "I really thought you'd be mad when you saw what we did to your car. How come you weren't?"

The question made her smile. "I was too stunned. I couldn't believe what I saw."

"I couldn't, either, when it happened," Luck admitted with a low chuckle. It reached out to share the moment of amusement with her and pulled her gaze in his direction.

With less wariness, Eve let herself forget their first meeting outside the tavern. There was an easy charm about Luck McClure that she found attractive, in addition to his looks. It had a quality of bold friendliness to it.

"Flirting" was a word that had a female connotation, but this was one time when Eve felt it could apply to a man without diminishing his virility. In fact, the gleam lurking in his blue eyes and the ready smile enhanced it. Part of her wished this was their first meeting, because she knew sooner or later he would recognize his "brown mouse." And a man like Luck McClure would never be attracted to a brown mouse.

His gaze slid from the road long enough to meet her eyes. There was warm male interest in the look that ran over her face, a look that probably had its basis in a curiosity similar to the one Eve had just experienced. She was briefly stimulated by it until she remembered how futile it was to be attracted to him. Eve glanced at the road a second before his attention returned to it.

"Our place is just ahead on the left," Eve stated.

As Luck slowed the car to make the turn into the short driveway, the boy, Toby, announced, "We go by here all the time. I didn't think anybody lived in that house. When did you move in?"

"This past weekend," she replied, then wondered if that would jog Luck's memory of the tavern incident. A quick glance didn't find any reaction. "We spend the summers here. We sometimes come here during the winter holidays to snowmobile or ice-fish and do some cross-country skiing."

"Do you like to ski?" Toby's questions continued even after the car stopped.

"With Mt. Telemark practically in our backyard, it would be a shame if I didn't." A faint smile touched her mouth as she shifted the sack of groceries to open the door. "As it happens, I enjoy it."

"Me, too. Dad took me skiing last Christmas." The boy scrambled out of the back seat to join his father. "Next year I'll be good enough to ski with him." He tipped his head back to look up at his father for confirmation. "Won't I, dad?"

"By the end of next winter, you'll be a veteran of the slopes," Luck agreed with a lazy smile, and waited until Eve had walked around the front of the car before starting toward the log cottage.

With this tall, good-looking man beside her, she felt oddly self-conscious—a sensation that had nothing to do with their previous encounter. It was more an awareness of physical attraction than an uneasiness. She failed to notice that Toby wasn't with them until the car door slammed again and the boy came running after them. Simultaneously she paused with Luck McClure to see what had delayed Toby.

"You left the keys in the ignition again, dad," the boy declared with an adult reprimand in his expression, and handed the car keys to his father. "That's how cars get stolen."

"Yes, Toby." Luck accepted the admonishment with lazy indulgence and slipped the keys into his pocket.

When they started toward the porch again, Toby tagged along.

Her parents recovered quickly from their initial surprise at the strange man and boy accom-

panying Eve into the house. She introduced
them, then Luck took over the explanation of
the shattered windshield. Exhibiting his typical
understanding, her father was not angered by
the accident. . . more amused than anything.

While they discussed particulars, Eve went
into the kitchen to put away the milk she'd got.
She remained in the alcove, satisfied to just
observe the easy way Luck McClure related to
her parents. It was a knack few people had. It
came naturally to him, part of his relaxed, easygoing style.

With all his apparent friendliness, Eve didn't
doubt that he could handle authority equally
well. There was something in his presence that
commanded respect. It was an understated quality, but that didn't lessen its strength.

Her gaze strayed to the boy standing beside
Luck. He was listening attentively to all that was
being said, possessing an oddly mature sense of
responsibility for a boy of his age. His only motion was tossing the ball into his glove and
retrieving it to toss it methodically again.

With the milk put away, Eve was running out
of reasons to dawdle in the kitchen. Since she
didn't want to take part in the conversation between her parents and Luck McClure, she took
her suntan lotion and shampoo and slipped
away to her bedroom. She paused in front of the
vanity mirror above her dresser and studied her
reflection.

The white band sleeked her brown hair away from her face, emphasizing features that were not so serene as they normally were. Eve touched the mouth that looked softer and fuller, fingertips brushing the curve. There was an added glow of suppressed excitement in the luminous brown of her eyes. The cause of it was Luck McClure and that never ending question of when he would recognize her.

With all the cheery yellow of her pants and top, Eve admitted to herself that she didn't look like a brown mouse. If anything, a sunflower was more apt—with its bright yellow petals and brown center.

"You really are a 'vanity' mirror," Eve murmured, and turned away from the reflecting glass before she became too wrapped up in her appearance.

But her subconscious made a silent resolution not to wear brown again. From now on, only bright colors would be added to her wardrobe. Drab clothing did nothing to improve her looks. "Brown mouse"—the phrase mocked her with its recollections of that night.

Eve dreaded the time when she would meet his wife, but in this small resort community it would be impossible for their paths not to cross sometime during the course of the summer. It would be foolish to try to avoid it. But what do you say to a woman whose husband tried to pick you up?

What kind of marriage did he have? He had said it was lonely at home and he wanted to talk to someone. He and his wife were obviously having trouble, Eve concluded. Or maybe he was just the type that stepped out anyway. No, she shook that thought away. Indulging in an idle flirtation would come naturally to him, but Luck McClure wasn't the type to let it go beyond the bantering of words. There was too much depth to him for that.

What did it matter? He was married. Regardless of the problems he was having, Luck was the kind who would persist until he solved them. It was ridiculous to waste her time thinking about a married man, no matter how interesting and compelling he might be.

The closing of the screen door and the cessation of voices from the front room turned Eve to face her bedroom door. She listened and heard the opening of car doors outside. The tall arresting man and his son were leaving.

It was just as well. Now she could come out of hiding—the realization stopped her short of the door. She had been hiding. Hiding because he had looked at her with a man's interest in the opposite sex and her ego hadn't wanted him to remember that she was a plain brown mouse. So what had she done? Scurried off into her hole, just like a brown mouse.

Never again, Eve resolved, and left her "hole" to return to the front room. The only occupant was her mother. Eve glanced around, noticing the Jaguar was gone from the drive-way.

"Where's dad?"

"Mr. McClure drove him back to the car. They called a garage. A man's coming over to pick up our car and replace the broken wind-shield," her mother explained. "He should be back shortly."

An hour later her father returned, but it was the mechanic who brought him back—not Luck McClure.

CHAPTER THREE

THE ROWLANDS were without transportation for two days. On the morning of the third day, the garage owner delivered the car, complete with a new windshield. The day had started out with gray and threatening skies. By the time the car was returned it began drizzling. And by noon it was raining steadily, confining Eve indoors.

With the car returned, her parents decided to restock their grocery supplies that afternoon. They invited Eve to come with them, but since they planned to visit some of their friends while they were out, she declined.

On rainy days she usually enjoyed curling up with a book, but on this occasion she was too restless to read. Since she had the entire afternoon on her hands, she decided to do some baking and went into the kitchen to stir up a batch of chocolate chip cookies, her father's favorite.

Soon the delicious smell of cookies baking in the oven filled the small cottage and chased away the gloom of the gray rainy day. Cookies from two sheet trays were cooling on the kitchen counter, atop an opened newspaper. Eve glanced through the glass door of the oven at the third sheet. Its cookies were just beginning to brown, a mere minute away from being done.

The thud of footsteps on the wooden porch floor reached her hearing, straightening Eve from the oven. An instant after they stopped, there was a knock on the door. She cast a glance at the oven, then went to answer the door. A splash of flour had left a white streak on the burgundy velour of her top. She brushed at it but only succeeded in spreading the white patch across her stomach. Eve was still brushing at it when she opened the door.

The slick material of a dark blue Windbreaker glistened with rain across a set of wide shoulders that turned at the sound of the opening door. Her hand stopped its motion when Eve looked into a pair of arresting blue eyes.

A tiny electric shock quivered through her nerve ends at the sight of Luck McClure on the other side of the wire mesh screen. Dampness gave a black sheen to his dark brown hair. Toby was beside him, his face almost lost under the hooded sweat shirt pulled over his head and tied under his chin. Beyond the shelter of the porch roof, rain fell in an obscuring gray curtain.

"Hello, Mr. McClure," Eve recovered her voice to greet him calmly.

An easy casual smile touched his mouth, so absently charming. "I stopped to—"

His explanation was interrupted by the oven timer dinging its bell to signal Eve the cookies should be done. "Excuse me. I have something in the oven." Manners dictated that she couldn't leave them standing on the porch, so she quickly unhooked the screen door. "Come in," she invited hurriedly, and retraced her path to the kitchen to remove the cookies before they burned.

Behind her she heard the screen door open and the shuffle of incoming footsteps. "Don't forget to wipe your feet, dad," Toby murmured the conscientious reminder.

Opening the oven door, Eve took a pot holder and used it to absorb the heat of the metal cookie sheet while she lifted it out of the oven. Another tray of individually spooned cookie dough was sitting on the counter, ready to be put in to bake. She slipped it on the rack with her free hand and closed the oven door.

"My parents are gone this afternoon." She said, carrying the sheet of baked cookies to the counter where the others were cooling, conscious that Luck McClure and his son had followed her to the kitchen. "Was there something I could help you with?" she offered, and began removing the cookies from the sheet with a metal spatula.

"I told your father he could use my car if he had any errands to run while his was in the shop," he explained. "I stopped to see if he needed it."

"The garage delivered our car this morning." Eve half turned to answer him and felt the slow inspection of his look.

Her cheeks were flushed from the heat of the oven. The sweep of his glance left behind an odd licking sensation that heightened her already high color. It was a look he would give to any semiattractive woman—a man's assessment of her looks—but that didn't alter its effect on her.

Toby appeared at her elbow, offering her a distraction. He peered over the top of the counter to see what she was doing. Untying his hood, he pushed it off his head, tousling his brown hair in the process.

"What are you making?" he said curiously.

"Chocolate-chip cookies." She smiled briefly at him and continued to slide the cookies off the flat spatula onto the newspaper with the rest.

He breathed in deeply, his blue eyes rounded as if drinking in the sight. "They smell good."

"Would you like one?" Eve offered. As an afterthought, she glanced at Luck, who had moved into her side vision. "Is it all right if he has a cookie?"

"Sure." Permission was granted with a faint nod of his head.

Toby reached for one that she had just set on the paper. "Careful," she warned, but it came too late. Toby was already jerking his hand away, nursing burned fingers.

"They're hot," he stated.

"Naturally. They just came out of the oven. Try one of those at the back." She pointed with the spatula. "They've had a chance to cool."

He took one of the cookies she'd indicated and bit into it. As he chewed it, he studied the cookie. "These are really good," he declared.

"You'll have to help your mother make some for you." Eve flashed him a smile at the compliment.

"I don't have a mother anymore," Toby replied absently, and took another bite of the cookie.

His statement sent invisible shock waves through her. She darted a troubled glance at Luck. Had his problems at home ended in divorce? Except for a certain blandness in his gaze, he didn't appear bothered by the topic his son had introduced.

"My wife died when Toby was small," he explained, and glanced at his son. The corners of his mouth were pulled upward in a smile. "Toby and I have been baching it for several years now, but I'm afraid our domestic talents don't stretch to baking cookies."

"I see," she murmured because she didn't know what else to say.

The knowledge that he was married, and therefore out of circulation, had made her feel safe from his obvious male attraction. The discovery that he was a widower caught her off guard, leaving her shaken.

"May I have another cookie?" Toby asked after he'd licked the melted chocolate of a chip from his finger.

"Of course." She'd made a large batch, so there was plenty to spare. Homemade cookies were obviously a special treat for the boy.

As he took another one, Toby glanced at his father. "Why don't you try one, dad? You don't know what you're missing."

"Go ahead." Eve added her permission and moved aside as she laid the last cookie down.

While Luck took her up on the offer and helped himself to a cookie, Eve carried the empty sheet to the adjoining counter and began spooning cookie dough onto it from the mixing bowl. The ever curious Toby followed her.

"What's that?"

"This is the cookie batter. When you bake it in the oven, it turns into a cookie." It was becoming obvious to her that this was all new to him. If he'd seen it before, it had been too long ago for him to remember clearly.

"How do you make it?" He looked up at her with a thoughtful frown.

"There's a recipe on the back of the chocolate-chip package." The teaching habit was too firmly ingrained for Eve to overlook the chance to impart knowledge when interest was aroused. She paused in her task to pick up the empty chip package and show it to him. "It's right there. It tells you all the ingredients and how to do it."

With the cookie in one hand and the package with its recipe in the other, Toby wandered to the opposite side of the kitchen and studied the printing with frowning concentration. The kitchen was a small alcove off the front room. When Luck moved to lean a hip against the counter near Eve, she began to realize how limited the walk space was.

"There is something very comfortable about a kitchen filled with the smell of fresh baking on a rainy day. It really feels like a home then," Luck remarked.

"Yes, it does," Eve agreed, and knew it was that casual intimacy that was disturbing her.

"Have you eaten one of your cookies? They *are* good," Luck said, confirming his son's opinion.

"Not yet," she admitted, and turned to tell him there was coffee in the electric pot if he wanted a cup. But when she opened her mouth to speak, he slipped the rounded edge of a warm cookie inside.

"A cook should sample her wares," he insisted with lazy inoffensive mockery.

There was an instant of surprised delay as her eyes met the glinting humor of his. Then her teeth instinctively sank into the sweet morsel to take a bite. Luck held onto the cookie until she did, then surrendered it to the hand that reached for it.

With food in her mouth, good manners dictated that she not speak until it was chewed and swallowed. It wasn't easy under his lazily watchful eyes, especially when he took due note of the tongue that darted out to lick the melted chocolate from her lips. Her heart began thumping against her ribs like a locomotive climbing a steep incline.

"I'll finish it later with some coffee." Eve set the half-eaten cookie on the counter, unwilling to go through the unnerving experience of Luck watching her eat again. She picked up the spoon and worked at concentrating on filling the cookie sheet with drops of dough.

"And I thought all along that Eve tempted Adam with an apple," Luck drawled softly. "When did you discover a cookie worked better?"

Again her gaze raced to him, surprised that he remembered her name and stunned by the implication of his words. No matter how she tried, Eve couldn't react casually to this sexual bantering of words the way he did. He was much more adept at the game than she was.

"What does 'tempted' mean?" Toby eyed his father curiously.

Luck turned to look at his son, not upset by the question nor the fact that Toby had been listening. "It's like putting a worm on a hook. The fish can't resist taking a nibble."

"Oh." With his curiosity satisfied, Toby's attention moved on to other things. He set the empty chocolate-chip package on the counter where Eve had left it before. "This doesn't look hard to do, dad. Do you think we could make some cookies sometime?"

"On the next rainy day we'll give it a try," he promised, and sent a twinkling look at Eve. "If we have trouble, we can give Eve a call."

"Yeah," Toby agreed with a wide grin.

Unexpectedly, just when Eve had decided Luck was going to become a fixture in the kitchen for what was left of the afternoon, he straightened from the counter. "Toby and I have taken advantage of your hospitality long enough. We'd better be leaving."

The timer went off to signal the other sheet of cookies was ready to come out of the oven. Its intrusive sound allowed her to turn away and hide the sudden rush of keen disappointment that he was leaving. It also permitted her to remember the reason for his visit.

"It was thoughtful of you to stop," Eve replied, taking the cookie sheet from the oven.

"It was the least I could do," Luck insisted, and paused in her path to the counter. She was compelled to look into the deep indigo color of his eyes. A half smile slanted his mouth. "I hope you have forgiven me for what happened the other time we met."

She went white with shock. "Then you do remember."

Although the smile remained, an attractive

frown was added to his expression. "I was talking about the broken windshield. Was there something else I was supposed to remember?"

She felt the curious intensity of his gaze probe for an answer, one that she had very nearly given away. "No. Of course not." She rushed a nervous smile onto her face and stepped around him to the counter, her pulse racing a thousand miles an hour.

For an uneasy moment, Eve thought he was going to question her answer, then she heard him take a step toward the front room and the door. "Tell your parents I said hello."

"I will," she promised, and turned when the pair were nearly to the door.

"Goodbye, Eve." Toby waved.

"Goodbye," she echoed his farewell.

The cottage seemed terribly quiet and empty after they'd gone. The gray rain outside the windows seemed to close in, its loneliness seeping in through the walls. Eve poured a cup of coffee and sat at the table to finish the cookie Luck had given her. It had lost some of its flavor.

THE FOLLOWING WEEK Eve volunteered to make the short trip to the store to buy bread, milk and the other essential items that always needed replenishing, so her parents could go boating with friends that had stopped by. When she arrived at the store, she was quick to notice the sleek Jaguar sedan parked in front of it. She wasn't aware of the glow of anticipation that came to her eyes.

Luck and Toby were on their way out of the store with an armful of groceries when she walked in. "Hello." Her bright greeting was a shade breathless.

The wide lazy smile that Luck gave her quickened her pulse. "You are safe today. Toby left his baseball and glove at the house," he said.

"Good. I was wondering whether I should stop here or not." Eve laughed as she lied, because she hadn't given the broken windshield incident another thought.

"Look what we bought." Toby reached into the smaller sack he carried and pulled out a package of chocolate chips. "We're going to make some the next time it rains."

"I hope they turn out," she smiled.

"So do I," Luck murmured dryly, and touched the boy's shoulder. "Let's go, Toby. We'll see you, Eve," he nodded, using that indefinite phrase that committed nothing.

"Bye, Eve."

The smile faded from her expression as she watched them go. Turning away from the door, she went to do her shopping.

"WHEN DO YOU SUPPOSE it's going to rain again?" Toby searched the blue sky for a glimpse of dark clouds, but there wasn't a sign of even a puffy white one. He sank to his knees on the beach towel that Luck was stretched out on. Grains of sand clung to his bare feet, wet like the rest of him from swimming in the lake. "It's been almost a week."

"Maybe we're in for a drought," Luck suggested with dry humor at his son's impatience.

"Very funny." Toby made a face at him and turned to squint into the sunlight reflected off the lake's surface. "The water is pretty warm. Are you going to come in for a swim now?"

"In a little bit." The heat of the sun burning into his exposed flesh made him lazy.

A red beach ball bounced on the sand near him and rolled onto his towel. Luck started to sit up and made it halfway before the ball's owner arrived.

"Sorry," a breathless female voice apologized.

Turning, he leaned on an elbow as a shapely blonde in a very brief bikini knelt on the sand beside him and reached for the ball. Her smile was wide and totally beguiling.

"No harm done," he assured her, and noticed the amount of cleavage that was revealed when she bent to pick up the ball.

His gaze lifted to her face and observed the knowing sparkle in her eyes. Wisely he guessed that it had all been a ploy to attract his attention. It was an old game. Despite the beautiful packaging, he discovered he wasn't interested in playing.

The blonde waited for several seconds, but he didn't make the expected gambit. Disappointment flickered in her expression, then was quickly veiled by a coy smile. Rising in a graceful turning motion, she ran back to her friends.

"That blonde was really a knockout, huh, dad?"

Amused, Luck cast a glance over his shoulder at his son, who was still staring after the shapely girl. "Yes, I guess she was," he agreed blandly, and looked back to the trio playing keep-away. Then he pushed himself into a full sitting position, his attention leaving the scantily clad blonde.

"She thought you were pretty neat, too," Toby observed, a hint of devilry in his smile. "I saw the sexy look she gave you."

"You see too much." Luck gave him a playful push backward, plopping him down on the sand.

Toby just laughed. "Why don't you marry someone like her?"

Luck sighed. He'd thought that subject had been forgotten. He shook his head in a mild form of exasperation. "Looks aren't everything, son." Rolling to his feet, he reached down to pull Toby up. "Let's go for that swim of yours."

"Race ya!" Toby challenged, and took off at a dead run.

He loped after him, his long strides keeping

the distance between them short. Wading into the lake until he was up to his knees, he then dived in. Powerful reaching strokes soon carried Luck into deeper water, where he waited for Toby to catch up with him.

"What do you think, pretty lady?" Luck murmured in a voice that was audible only to himself. "Have you ruined me for anyone else?"

The image of his wife swirled through the mists of his mind, her face laughing up at him as she pulled him to their bed. Her features were soft, like a fading edge of a dream, her likeness no longer bringing him the sharp stabbing pain. Time had reduced it to a beautiful memory that came back to haunt him at odd times.

Although he still possessed a man's sexual appetite, emotional desire seemed to have left him. Except for Toby, it seemed that all the good things in life were behind him. Tomorrow seemed empty, without promise.

A squeal of female laughter from the lakeshore pulled his gaze to the beach and the cavorting blonde. Her bold bid for his attention had left him cold, even though he had liked what he had seen. He found the subtle approach much sexier—like the time Eve had licked the chocolate from her lips. Strange that he had thought of her instead of the way his wife, Lisa, used to run her finger around the rim of a glass.

A hand sprayed water on his face. Luck

blinked and wiped the droplets from his eyes as
Toby laughed and struck out, swimming away
from him. The moment of curious reflection
was gone as he took up the challenge of his son.

THUNDER CRASHED AND ROLLED across the sky,
unleashing a torrent of rain to hammer on the
roof of the cottage. A rain-cool breeze rushed in
through a window above the kitchen sink, stir-
ring the brown silk of Eve's hair as she washed
the luncheon dishes.

Lightning cracked outside the window. "My,
that looked close," her mother murmured,
always a little nervous about violent storms.

"The baseball game in Milwaukee has just
been postponed because of the rain," her father
sighed in disappointment and switched off the
radio atop the refrigerator. "And they always
have doubleheaders on Saturday, too." If her
father had one passion besides fishing, it was
baseball. "Maybe it will clear off later this
afternoon and—" He was interrupted by the
ring of the telephone in the front room. "I'll get
it."

"If it's Mabel and Frank, tell them to come
over," her mother called. "It's a good day to
play cards."

On the third ring, he answered it. "It's for
you, Eve." He had to raise his voice to make
himself heard above the storm.

Grabbing a towel, Eve wiped the dishwater

from her hands as she walked to the phone. "Hello?"

"Hello, Eve. This is Toby. Toby McClure."

A vague surprise widened her eyes. "Hello, Toby." Warm pleasure ran through her voice and expression.

"I'm trying to make some chocolate-chip cookies," he said, and she smiled when she remembered this was the first rainy day since he and Luck had been over. "But I can't figure out how to get cream from shortening and sugar."

"What?" A puzzled frown creased her forehead as she tried to fathom his problem.

"The directions say to 'cream' the sugar and shortening," Toby explained patiently.

Eve swallowed the laugh that bubbled in her throat. The directions probably didn't make sense to him. "That means you should blend them together until they make a thick 'creamy' mixture."

A heavy sigh came over the phone. "I thought this was going to be easy, but it isn't." There was a pause, followed by a reluctant request, "Eve, I don't suppose you could maybe come over and show me how to make them?" There was so much pride in his voice, and a grudging admission of defeat.

"Where's your father? He should be able to help you," she suggested.

"He didn't get home until real late last night,

so he's lying down, taking a nap," Toby explained. "Can you come?"

It was impossible to turn him down, especially when she didn't want to. "Yes, I'll come. Where exactly do you live?" Eve knew it was somewhere close from other comments that had been made. Toby gave her precise directions. After she had promised to be there within a few minutes, she hung up the phone. "Dad, were you or mom planning to use the car this afternoon?"

"No. Did you want to use it?" He was already reaching in his pocket for the keys.

"I'm off to the McClures to give Toby his first lesson in baking cookies," Eve explained with a soft laugh, and told them the boy's problem understanding the directions. Their amusement blended with hers.

"Never mind the dishes. I'll finish them," her mother volunteered. "You'd better take an umbrella, too, and wear a coat."

In her bedroom, Eve brushed her hair and freshened her lipstick. She didn't allow herself to wonder why she was taking so much trouble with her appearance when she was going to see an eight-year-old. It would have started her thinking about his father, something she was trying to pretend not to do at this point. She hesitated before taking the brown coat out of her closet, but it was the only one she had that repelled water.

The sheeting rain was almost more than the windshield wipers could handle. It obscured her vision so that, despite Toby's excellent directions, she nearly missed the turn into the driveway. The lake house was set back in the trees, out of sight of the road. Eve parked her car behind the Jaguar.

The umbrella afforded her little protection from the driving rain. Her coat was stained wet by the time she walked the short distance from the car to the front door. Toby must have been watching for her, because he opened the door a second before she reached it. He pressed a forefinger to his lips and motioned her inside. She hurried in, unable to do anything about the rainwater dripping from her and the umbrella.

"Dad's still sleeping," Toby whispered, and explained, "He needs the rest."

The entry hall skirted the living room, paneled in cedar with a heavy beamed slanted ceiling and a natural stone fireplace. Toby's glance in that direction indicated it was where Luck was sleeping. Eve looked in when Toby led her past. There, sprawled on a geometric-patterned couch, was Luck, naked from the waist up, an arm flung over his head in sleep. It was the first time Eve had ever seen anyone frowning in his sleep.

In the kitchen, Toby led her to the table where he had all the ingredients set out. "Will you show me how to make cookies?" he asked, repeating the request he'd made over the phone.

"No, I won't show you," Eve said, taking off her wet coat and draping it over a chair back. "I'll tell you how to do it. The best way to learn is by doing."

Step by step, she directed him through the mixing process. When the first sheet came out of the oven, Toby was all eyes. He could hardly wait until the cookies were cool enough to taste and, thus, assure himself that they were as good as they looked.

"They taste just like yours," he declared on a triumphant note after he'd taken the first bite.

"Of course," Eve laughed, but kept it low so she wouldn't waken Luck in the next room.

"I couldn't have done it if you hadn't helped me," Toby added, all honesty. "You're a good teacher."

"That's what I am. Really," she emphasized when he failed to understand. "I *am* a teacher."

"What subject?"

"Music."

"Too bad it isn't English. That's my worst subject," he grimaced. "Dad isn't very good at it, either."

"We all have subjects that we don't do as well in as others," Eve shrugged lightly. "Mine is math."

"Dad is really good at that, and science, but he has to use it all the time in his work."

"What does he do?"

"He works for my grandpa." Then realizing that didn't answer her question, Toby elaborated, "My grandpa owns North Lakes Lumber. Mostly my dad works on the logging side. That way we can spend more time together in the summer when I'm out of school. He had a meeting with grandpa last night. That's why he was so late coming home."

"I thought he had a date." The words were out before Eve realized she had spoken.

"Sometimes he goes out on dates," Toby admitted, finding nothing wrong with her comment. "We like going places and doing things together, but sometimes dad is like me. I like to play with kids my own age once in a while; so does he. I imagine you do, too."

"Yes, that's true." She silently marveled at his logical reasoning. He was quite a remarkable boy.

Without being reminded, he checked on the cookies in the oven and concluded they were done. He took the cookie sheet out with a pot holder and rested it on the tabletop while he scooped the cookies off.

"We've been talking about dad getting married again," he announced, and didn't see the surprised arch of her eyebrow. "Dad gets pretty lonely sometimes. It's been rough on him since my mother died six years ago. Three weeks ago it was six years *exactly*," he stressed, and shook his head in a rueful fashion when he looked at her. "Boy, did he ever go on a binge that night!" He rolled his eyes to emphasize the point.

Three weeks ago. Eve did a fast mental calculation, her mind whirling. "Was...that on a Thursday?"

"I think so. Why?" Toby eyed her with an unblinking look.

The night she'd bumped into him outside the tavern. He had wanted someone to talk to, Eve remembered. A man can talk to a brown mouse, Luck had said. But she had refused, and he had gone back inside the tavern.

"No reason." She shook her head absently. "It was nothing important." But she couldn't resist going back to the subject. "You said he got drunk that night." She tried to sound mildly interested.

"I guess," Toby agreed emphatically. "He even had hallucinations."

"He did?"

"After I helped him into bed, he claimed that he had talked to a brown mouse." He looked at her, laughter suddenly dancing in his eyes. "Can you imagine that?"

"Yes." Eve swallowed and tried to smile. "Yes, I can." Her suspicions were confirmed beyond question. Now she wanted off the subject. "I'll help you spoon the cookie dough on the tray," she volunteered, letting action take the place of words.

When the last sheet of cookies came out of the oven, Eve washed the baking dishes while Toby wiped them and put them away. He leaned an elbow on the counter and watched her scrub at the baked-on crumbs on the cookie sheet.

"I don't really mind helping with dishes, or even making my bed," Toby said, and propped his head up with his hand. "But I'm going to like having a mother."

She didn't see the connection between the two statements. "Why is that?"

"Because sometimes my friends tease me when I have to dust furniture or fold clothes," he explained. "Dad told me that mothers clean and cook and do all those kinds of things."

"That's true." Eve tried very hard not to smile. It had to be rough to have your manhood questioned by your peers when you were only eight years old. Reading between the lines, she could see where Toby had acquired his air of maturity. Responsibility had been given to him at an early age, so he didn't possess that carefree attitude typical of most children his age.

She rinsed the last cookie sheet and handed it to Toby to dry. Draining the dishwater from the sink, she wiped off the counter, then dried her hands. She glanced at the wall clock and wondered where the afternoon had gone.

"Now that we have everything cleaned up, it's time I was leaving," she declared.

"Can't you stay a little while longer?"

"No, it's late." She removed her brown coat from the chair back and slipped it on.

Toby brought her the umbrella. "Thanks for coming, Eve." He stopped for an instant as a thought occurred to him. "Maybe I should call you Miss Rowland, since you're a teacher."

"I'd like it better if you called me Eve," she replied, and started toward the entry hall.

"Okay, Eve," he grinned, and walked with her.

As she passed the living room, her gaze was automatically drawn inside. Luck was sitting up, rubbing his hands over his face as though he had just wakened. The movement in front of him attracted his attention. He glanced up and became motionless for an instant when he saw Eve.

Because of the clouds blocking out the sun, there was little light in the entry way. Eve didn't think about the dimness as she started to speak, smiling at the grogginess that was evident in his expression.

But Luck spoke before she did. "Don't scurry off into the darkness...brown mouse." There was a trancelike quality to his voice.

Her steps faltered. She had escaped recognition for so long that she had stopped dreading it. Now that he remembered her, she felt sick. Tearing her gaze from him, she hurried toward the front door. As she jerked it open, she heard him call her name.

"Eve!"

She didn't stop. She didn't even remember to open the umbrella until the slow rain drenched her face. There was water on the ground. It splashed beneath her running feet as she hurried toward her car.

CHAPTER FOUR

A STARTLED OUTCRY was torn from her throat by the hand that caught her arm and spun her around. Eve hadn't thought Luck would come after her—not out in the rain. But there he was, standing before her with his naked chest glistening a hard bronze from the rain, the sprinkling of chest hairs curling tightly in the wetness. The steady rain beat at his dark hair, driving it onto his forehead. Reluctantly, Eve lifted her gaze to the blue of his eyes, drowning in the full recognition of his look.

"You *are* the girl I bumped into outside the tavern that night," Luck stated in final acceptance of the fact.

"Yes." The hand holding the umbrella wavered, causing Luck to dodge his head and duck under the wire spines stretching the material.

His gaze swept her face, hair and eyes. "I thought I'd conjured you out of a whiskey bottle. I don't know why nothing clicked when I met you." A frown flickered between his brows, then vanished when his gaze slid to her coat. "It must have been the combination of the shadows

and the brown coat...and the fogginess of
sleep. Why didn't you say anything before?''

"And remind you that I was the brown
mouse?'' There was bitterness in the laughing
breath she released.

"What's wrong with being a brown mouse?''
The corners of his mouth deepened in an attractive smile. "I recall that I happened to like the
brown mouse I met.''

"A brown mouse is just a small rat. It's hardly a name that someone wants to be called.''
This time Eve worked to keep the bitterness out
of her voice and turn the comment into a joke
for her pride's sake. She succeeded to a large
degree. "You certainly don't want to remind
someone of it if they've forgotten.''

"It's all in the eye of the beholder, Eve,''
Luck corrected with a rueful twist of his mouth.
"You see a rat, and I see a soft furry creature.
You are a strong sensitive woman, but you
aren't very sure of yourself. I wish you had
stayed that night. It all might have turned out
differently.''

How could she say that she wished she had,
too, knowing what she knew now. Hindsight
always altered a person's perspective.

"Dad!'' Toby shouted from the opened front
door. "You'd better come inside! You're getting soaking wet out there!''

"Toby's right.'' Her gaze fell to the rivulets
of rainwater running down the muscled con-

tours of his bare chest, all hard sinew and taut sun-browned skin. His blatant maleness spun a whole new set of evocative sensations. "You're getting drenched. You should go in the house."

"Come in with me." Luck didn't let go of her arms, holding her as he issued the invitation.

"No. I have to go home." She resisted the temptation to accept, listening to the steady drip of rain off her umbrella, its swift fall in the same rhythm as her pulse.

His mouth quirked. "That's what you said then, too."

"It's late. I—" The sentence went no farther as the wetness of his palm cupped her cheek. Eve completely forgot what she was going to say, her thoughts scattered by the disturbing caress of his touch.

"Dad!" Toby sounded impatient and irritated. "You're going to catch your death of pneumonia!"

It was the diversion Eve needed to collect her senses before she did something foolish. "You'd better go." She turned away, breaking contact with his hand and lifting the umbrella high enough to clear his head. There was no resistance as she slipped out of his grasp to walk the last few steps to the car.

"We'll see you again, Eve." It was a definite statement.

But she wasn't certain what promise it contained. "Yes." She opened the car door and slipped inside, struggling to close the wet umbrella. Luck continued to stand in the rain, watching her.

"Do you think it will be sunny tomorrow?" he asked unexpectedly.

"I haven't been paying any attention to the weather forecast," Eve replied.

"Neither have I," Luck admitted.

HE WAS INDIFFERENT to the slow rain falling on him as he watched Eve reverse the car at a right angle to turn around in the drive. The incident had not been a figment of an alcoholic imagination. The woman he'd thought he had only dreamed about had actually been under his nose all this time.

The one good feeling he'd experienced in six years had happened when he had held her in his arms, but he hadn't believed it was real. Even now Luck wasn't sure that part hadn't been imagined. Comfortable didn't describe the feeling it had aroused. It was something more basic than that. It had been right and natural with his arms around her, feeling the softness of her body against his.

The woman had been Eve. It was strange he hadn't realized it before. She was quiet and warm, with an inner resiliency and a gentle humor that he liked. A smile twitched his mouth as Luck remembered she had a definite will of her own, as well. She wasn't easily intimidated.

"Dad!"

He turned, letting his gaze leave the red tail-lights of her car, and walked to the house, wet feet squishing in wet shoes. A smile curved his mouth at the disapproving expression on his son's face when he reached the door.

"You're sopping wet," Toby accused. "You wouldn't let me run out there like that with no coat or anything. You tell me I'll catch cold. How come you can do it?"

"Because I'm stupid," Luck replied, because he couldn't argue with the point his son had raised.

"You'd better get out of those wet clothes," Toby advised.

"I intend to." He left a watery trail behind him as he walked to the private bath off his bedroom where he stripped and put on the toweling robe Toby brought him. "Why was Eve here?" he asked, vigorously rubbing his wet hair with a bath towel.

"She came over to help me make cookies. They're good, too." A sharp questioning glance from Luck prompted Toby to explain. "I called and asked her to come over 'cause I was having trouble with the directions and you were asleep." Then it was his turn to tip his head to one side and send a questioning look at his father. "How come you called her a brown mouse?"

"It turns out Eve was the one I talked to that

night and referred to as a brown mouse," he shrugged, and tossed the towel over a rack.

"I thought you were drunk that night."

"I had a few drinks, more after I met her than before. Which probably explains why I wasn't sure whether it had happened or I had imagined it."

"But why did you call her a brown mouse?" Toby didn't understand that yet.

"It's a long story," Luck began.

"I know," Toby inserted with a resigned sigh. "You'll tell me all about it some other time."

"That's right." A smile played with the corners of his mouth as he turned his son around and pushed him in front of him out of the bathroom. "Is there any coffee made?"

"Yeah." Toby tilted his head way back to frown at him. "I just hope you remember all the things you're going to tell me 'some other time.'"

In the kitchen, Luck filled a mug with coffee and helped himself to a handful of the cookies stacked on the table. "What did you and Eve talk about?" Settling onto a chair, he bit into one of the cookies and eyed Toby skeptically. "Did you really make these?"

"Yeah," was the defensive retort. "Eve told me how. She says you learn best by doing. She's a teacher. Did you know that? I mean a for-real teacher. She teaches music."

"No, I didn't know that," Luck admitted.

"We talked about that some and a bunch of other things." Toby frowned in an attempt to recall the subjects he'd discussed with Eve. "I told her you were thinking about getting married again."

Luck choked on the drink of coffee he'd taken and coughed, "You did what?!!" He set the mug down to stare at his son, controlling the anger that trembled beneath his disbelieving look.

"I mentioned that you were talking about getting married again," he repeated with all the round-eyed innocence of an eight-year-old. "Well, it's true."

"No, *you've* been talking about it." Luck pointed a finger at his son, shaking it slightly in his direction. "Why on earth did you mention it to Eve? I thought it was a private discussion between you and me."

"Gosh, dad, I didn't know you wanted to keep it a secret," Toby blinked.

"Toby, you don't go around discussing personal matters with strangers." He ran his fingers through his damp hair in a gesture of exasperation. "My God, you'll be blabbing it to the whole neighborhood next. Why don't you just take an ad out in the paper? Wanted: A wife for a widower with an eight-year-old blabbermouth."

"Do you think anyone would apply?" Behind

the thoughtful frown, there was the beginnings
of a plan.

"No!" Luck slammed his hand on the table.
"If I find out that you've put an advertisement
in any paper, I swear you won't be able to sit
down for a week! This marriage business has
gone far enough!"

"But you said—" Toby started to protest.

"I don't care what I said," Luck interrupted
with a slicing wave of his hand to dismiss that
argument. "I've played along with this marriage
idea of yours, but it's got to stop. I'll decide
when and *if* I'm getting married again without
any prompting from you!"

"But face it, dad, you should get married,"
Toby patiently insisted. "You need somebody
to keep you company and to look after you. I'm
getting too old to be doing all this woman's
work around the house."

"You don't get married just for companionship and someone to keep house." Luck regretted his earlier, imprecise explanation of a
mother's role. It had started this whole mess.
"There is more involved than that. A man is
supposed to love the woman he marries."

"You're talking about hugging and kissing
and that stuff," Toby nodded in understanding.

"That and...other things," Luck conceded
with marked impatience.

"You mean sex, like in that book you and I
read together when you explained to me how

babies were made," his son replied quite calmly.

Luck shook his head and scratched his forehead. "Yes, I mean sex and the feelings you have toward the woman you marry."

"Would you consider marrying someone like Eve?" Toby cocked his head at a wondering angle. "You said looks weren't everything."

"Why did you say a thing like that?" he challenged with irritation. "Don't you think Eve is an attractive woman?"

"Eve is all right, I like her, but—"

"No buts!" Luck flashed. "Eve is a lovely young woman and I don't want you implying otherwise with comments like 'looks aren't everything.' It's thoughtless remarks like that that hurt people's feelings." He should know. He had already wounded Eve when he called her a brown mouse, even though he hadn't meant it to be unkind. "Don't ever say anything to slight her!"

"Gee, dad, you don't have to get so hostile," Toby admonished, and defended his position. "Eve just doesn't look anything at all like the blonde we saw on the beach the other day. That blonde could have been the centerfold in *Playboy* magazine."

Luck started to ask where Toby had gotten his hands on a magazine like that, but he remembered his own curiosity at that age and decided not to pursue the issue at this time. Instead he just sighed, "I'm not interested in marrying a woman who has staples in her stomach."

Toby jerked his head and frowned. "Why would she have staples in her stomach?"

"Never mind." He lifted his hands in defeat. "The whole subject of women and marriage is closed. But you remember what I said about Eve," he warned. "I don't want to hear you making any disparaging remarks about her."

"I wouldn't, dad." Toby looked offended. "She's nice."

"Don't forget it, then," he replied less forcefully, and stood up. "I'm going to get out of this robe and put some clothes on. You'd better find something to put these cookies in."

"Yes, sir," Toby agreed in a dispirited tone.

Luck hesitated. "I didn't mean to be rough on you, Toby. I know you mean well. It's just that sometimes you make situations very awkward without realizing it."

"How?"

"I can't explain." He shook his head, then reached out to rumple his son's hair in a show of affection. "Don't let it worry you."

THE RAIN had washed the land clean. The sky was a fresh clear blue while the green pine needles had lost their coat of dust to contrast sharply with the blue horizon. After a day's worth of summer sunshine, the ground was dry-ing out, with only water standing in the low spots as a reminder it had rained.

Sitting on the seat in front of the upright piano, Eve let her fingers glide over the keys, seeking out the Mozart melody without conscious direction. She played from memory, eyes closed, listening to the individual notes flowing from one to another. The beauty of the song was an indirect therapy for the vague dejection that had haunted her since Luck had recognized her as his brown mouse less than two days ago.

When the last note faded into the emptiness of the cottage, Eve reluctantly let her fingers slide from the keys to her lap. The applause from a single person sounded behind her. Startled, Eve swung around on the piano seat to discover the identity of her audience of one.

The wire mesh of the screen door darkened the form of the man standing on the porch, but Eve recognized Luck instantly. An alternating pleasure and uncertainty ran through her system, setting her nerves on edge while quickening her pulse.

"I didn't hear you come." She rose quickly to cross the room and unhook the door. "Mom and dad went fishing this morning." As she pushed open the door to let him in, she noticed the only car in the driveway belonged to her parents. "Where's your car?"

"I came by boat." He stepped inside, so tall and so vigorously manly. Eve kept a safe distance between them to elude the raw force of his attraction that seemed to grow stronger with each meeting. "I tied it up at the shore. Toby's watching it."

"Oh." The knack of idle conversation deserted her. It was foolish to let that brown-mouse episode tie her tongue, but it had. She should never have allowed herself to become so sensitive about it. She should have accepted Luck's explanation the other day and let it die.

"Toby and I decided to take a ride around the lake this morning and thought you might like to come along." That lazy half smile that Eve found so disturbing accompanied his invitation.

Her delight was short-lived as she read between the lines. "It's thoughtful of you to ask, but I don't want you to feel that you're obligated to do so because you think you should make up for what happened outside the tavern that night." There was a trace of pride in the way she held her head, tipped higher than normal.

His smile grew more pronounced, bringing a gentleness to his hard-hewn features. "I'm not going to apologize for anything I said or did then," Luck informed her. "I regret that you felt slighted by the phrase of brown mouse, but I meant it in the kindest possible way. I'm asking you to come with us because we'd like your company. If you feel that I need an excuse to ask, then let's say that it is my way of thanking

you for showing Toby how to make cookies."
Glinting blue eyes gently mocked her as he
paused. "Will you cóme with us?"

Eve smiled in a self-mocking way that etched
attractive dimples in her cheeks. "I'd like to,
yes," she accepted. "Just give me a couple of
minutes to change." It would be too awkward
climbing in and out of a boat in the wraparound
denim skirt she was wearing.

"Sure." He reached for the screen door to
open it. "We'll be stopping for lunch, probably
at one of the resorts along the lake."

Eve hesitated, wondering if she was being too
presumptuous, then threw caution to the wind
to suggest, "If you'll give me another fifteen
minutes, I can fix some sandwiches and stuff for
a picnic lunch. Toby would like that."

"Toby would love it," Luck agreed. "We'll
meet you at the boat in fifteen minutes."

"I'll be there," she promised as he pushed the
door open and walked out.

Lingering near the door, Eve watched him de-
scend the steps and strike out across the road
toward the lakeshore, a warm feeling of pleasure running swiftly through her veins. Before
he had disappeared from view, she retreated to
the kitchen to take the picnic basket out of the
pantry cupboard and raid the refrigerator. To
go with the ham sandwiches she fixed, Eve added a wedge of Wisconsin Cheddar cheese along
with some milder Colby, plus crackers and red

Delicious apples. She filled a thermos cooler with lemonade and packed it in the basket, then laid a bag of potato chips on top.

Most of the allotted time was gone when she entered her bedroom. She quickly changed out of the skirt and blouse into a pair of white shorts and a flame-red halter top. At the last minute, she slipped on a pair of white canvas shoes with rubber soles and grabbed a long-sleeved blouse from the closet, in case she wanted protection from the sun.

With her arm hooked through the handle of the picnic basket, Eve crossed the road to the lake. Toby was skipping stones across the flat surface of the lake, a picture of intensity. A cigarette dangled from Luck's mouth, his eyes squinting against the curling smoke as he stood in a relaxed stance beside his son. At the sound of Eve's approach, the upper half of his body swiveled toward her. His gaze swept her in slow appreciation, setting her aglow with pleasure.

"Hi, Eve!" Toby greeted her with an exuberant welcome, the handful of stones falling from his hands so he could brush the dust from them.

"You still have two minutes to go." Luck dropped the cigarette to the ground, grinding it dead under his heel.

"Maybe I should go back to the cottage," Eve laughed in a suddenly buoyant mood.

"Oh, no, you don't," Luck denied the suggestion, a matching humor shining in his look.

She surrendered the picnic basket to his reaching hand. A line tied around a tree moored the pleasure cruiser close to the shore. Luck swung the basket onto the bow, then turned to help Eve aboard. Previously she had only guessed at the strength in the sinewed muscles of his shoulders and arms. But when his hands spanned the bareness of her rib cage and lifted her with muscles rippling to swing her up onto the bow as easily as he had the basket, she had her belief confirmed.

The imprint of his firm hands stayed with her, warming her flesh and letting her relive the sensation of his touch as she carried the basket to the stern of the boat and stowed it under one of the cushioned seats. Toby was tossed aboard with equal ease and came scrambling back to where Eve was. After untying the mooring line, Luck pushed the boat into deeper water and heaved himself on board.

"All set?" Luck cast them each a glance as his hand paused on the ignition key.

At their nods, he turned the key. The powerful engine of the cruise boat sputtered, then roared smoothly to life, the blades churning water. Turning the wheel, Luck maneuvered the boat around to point toward the open water before opening the throttle to send it shooting forward.

The speed generated a wind that lifted the swath of brown hair from Eve's neck, blowing and swirling it behind her. A little late she realized she hadn't brought a scarf. There was nothing to be done about it now, so she turned her face to the wind, letting it race over her and whip the hair off her shoulders.

Resting her arm on the side of the boat, Eve had a clear view of all that was in front of her, including Luck. He stood behind the wheel, his feet braced apart. The sun-bronzed angles of his jutting profile were carved against a blue sky as vividly blue as his eyes. The wind ruffled the virile thickness of his dark hair and flattened his shirt against his hard flesh, revealing the play of muscles beneath it. Snug Levi's outlined the slimness of his hips and the corded muscles of his thighs, reinforcing an aura of rough sexiness. Something stirred deep within her.

The instant Eve realized how openly she was staring, she shifted her gaze to the boy at his side, a youthful replica of his father. This day Toby had left behind his mask of maturity to adopt the carefree attitude that was usually so evident in Luck with that dancing glint in his eyes and easy smile.

The loud throb of the engine made conversation impossible, but Eve heard Toby urge his father to go faster. She saw the smile Luck flashed him and knew he laughed, even though the wind stole the sound from her. The throttle was pushed wide open until the powerboat was skimming over the surface of the water and bouncing over the wakes of other boats as the churning blades sent out their own fantail.

Luck glanced over at her and smiled, and Eve smiled back. For a brief moment, she allowed herself to consider the intimate picture they made—man, woman and child. For an even briefer minute, she let herself pretend that that's the way it was, until realism caught her up sharply and made her shake the image away.

After a while, Luck eased the throttle back and turned the wheel over to his son. Toby swelled with importance, his oversized sense of responsibility surfacing to turn his expression serious. Luck stayed beside him the first few minutes until Toby got the feel of operating the boat. Then he moved to the opposite side of the boat to lean a hip against the rail and keep an unobtrusive vigil for traffic that his son might not see. The position put him almost directly in front of Eve.

His sweeping side-glance caught her looking at him and Luck raised his voice to comment, "It's a beautiful day."

"Lovely," Eve shouted the agreement, because it did seem perfect to her. The wind made an unexpected change of direction and blew the hair across her face. Turning her head, she pushed it away. When she looked back, Luck was facing the front.

A quarter of an hour later or more, he straightened and motioned to her. "It's your turn to be skipper!" Luck called.

"Aye, aye, sir," she grinned, and moved to relieve Toby at the wheel.

She was quick to notice that the small boy was just beginning to show the tension of operating the boat. Wisely Luck had seen it and had Eve take over before it ceased to be fun for Toby and became onerous instead. Out of the corner of her eye, Eve saw Toby dart over to receive praise from his father for a job well done. Then her attention was centered on guiding the boat.

Luck said something to her, but the wind and the engine noise tore it away. She shook her head and frowned that she didn't hear him. He crossed over to stand in a small space behind her.

"Let's go to the northern side of the lake," he leaned forward to repeat his suggestion.

"I'm not familiar with that area. We don't usually go up that far." Eve half turned her head to answer him and discovered he had bent closer to hear her, which brought his face inches from hers. Her gaze touched briefly on his mouth, then darted swiftly to his eyes to be captured by their vivid blueness.

"Neither am I. Let's explore strange waters together," Luck replied, his eyes crinkling at the corners.

"Okay." But there was a breathless quality to her voice.

It was some minutes after she turned the boat north before Luck abandoned his post behind her. It was only when he was gone that Eve realized how overly conscious she had been of his closeness, every nerve end tingling, although no contact had been made.

Familiar territory was left behind as they ventured into unknown waters. When a cluster of islands appeared, Eve reduced the boat's speed to find the channel through them. She hesitated over the choice.

"Want me to take over?" Luck asked.

"Yes." She relinquished the wheel to him with a quick smile. "That way if you run into a submerged log, it will be your fault instead of mine."

"Wise thinking," he grinned.

"Look!" Toby shouted, and pointed toward the waters ahead of them. "It's a deer swimming across the lake."

In the lake waters off their port side, there was the antlered head of a young buck swimming across the span of water between two islands. Luck throttled the engine to a slow idle, so they could watch him. When the deer reached the opposite island, it scrambled onto shore and disappeared within seconds in the thick stand of trees and underbrush.

"Boy, that was really something, huh, dad?" Toby exclaimed.

"It sure was," was the indulgent agreement.

With a child's lightning change of subject, Toby asked, "When are we going to have our picnic?"

"When we get hungry," Luck replied.

"I'm hungry," Toby stated.

Luck glanced at his watch. "I guess we can start looking for a place to go ashore. Or would you rather drop anchor and eat on the boat?" He included Eve in the question.

"It doesn't matter to me," she shrugged.

"Maybe we can land on one of the islands," Toby suggested.

"I don't know why not," Luck smiled down at the boy, then began surveying the cluster of islands for a likely picnic spot.

"Who knows? Maybe we'll find Chief Namekagon's lost silver mine," Eve remarked.

Toby turned to her. "What lost silver mine?"

"The one that belonged to the Indian chief the lake was named after. Legend has it that it's on one of the islands on the lake," she explained.

"Is it true?" Toby frowned.

"No one knows for sure," she admitted. "But he paid for all his purchases at the trading post in Ashland with pure silver ore. Supposedly the old chief was going to show the location of his mine to a friend, but he saw a bad omen and postponed the trip. Then he died without ever telling anyone where it was."

"Wow!" Toby declared with round-eyed excitement. "Wouldn't it be something if we found it?"

"A lot of people have looked over the years," Eve cautioned. "No one has found it yet."

"How about having our picnic there?" Luck pointed to an island with a wide crescent of sand stretching in front of its pine trees.

"It looks perfect." Eve approved the choice, and Luck nosed the boat toward the spot.

CHAPTER FIVE

THE THREE OF THEM sat cross-legged on a blanket Luck had brought from the boat while Eve unpacked the picnic basket. "Cheese, fruit, crackers," Luck said, observing the items she removed. "All that's missing is a bottle of wine. You should have said something."

There were too many romantic overtones in that remark. Eve wasn't sure how to interpret it, so she tried the casual approach and reached in the basket for the cold thermos.

"I guess we'll have to make do with lemonade," she shrugged brightly.

"I like lemonade," Toby inserted as she set the thermos aside to arrange a sandwich and a portion of chips on a paper plate and handed it to him. "This looks good, Eve."

"I hope you like it." She fixed a plate for Luck, then one for herself, leaving the cheese, fruit and crackers on top of the basket for dessert.

"Have you ever looked for the lost mine, Eve?" Toby munched thoughtfully on his sandwich while he studied her.

"Not really. Just a few times when I was your age."

The subject continued to fascinate him. Throughout the meal, he pumped her for information, dredging up tidbits of knowledge Eve had forgotten she knew. Toby refused the slice of cheese she offered him when his sandwich was gone but took the shiny apple.

Luck ate his. When it was gone, he used the knife to slice off another chunk. "This is good cheese."

"Wisconsin cheese, of course," she smiled. "Anything else would be unpatriotic."

"Did Chief Namekagon really have seven wives?" Toby returned to his favorite subject.

"Yes, but I guess he must have kept the location of the mine a secret from them, too," Eve replied.

"Seven wives," Toby sighed, and glanced at his father. "Gee, dad, all you need is one."

"Or none," Luck murmured softly, and sent a look of silencing sharpness at his son. "More lemonade, Toby?"

"No, thanks." He tossed his apple core into the small sack Eve had brought along for their wastepaper. Rising, Toby dusted the sandwich crumbs from his legs. "Is it okay if I do a little exploring?"

At Luck's nod of permission, Toby took off. Within minutes, he had disappeared along a faint animal path that led into the island's thick forest. For the first few minutes, they could hear him rustling through the underbrush. When that stopped, Eve became conscious of the silence and that she was alone with Luck. Her gaze strayed to him, drawn by an irrepressible compulsion, only to have her heart knock against her ribs when she found him watching her.

"More cheese?" She spoke quickly to cover the sudden disturbance that seethed through her. In the far distance, there was the sound of a boat traversing the lake, reminding her they weren't the only ones in the vicinity, no matter how isolated they seemed.

"No. I'm full." Luck shook his dark head in refusal.

Inactivity didn't suit her at the moment because she knew it would take her thoughts in a direction that wasn't wise. "I'd better pack all this away before it attracts all the insects on the island."

Eve tightly wrapped the cheese that was left and stowed it in the basket with the thermos of lemonade and the few potato chips that were left. As she added the paper sack with their litter to the basket, she was conscious that Luck had risen. When he crouched beside her, balanced on the balls of his feet, she found it diffcult to breathe normally. His warm scent was all around her, heightened by the heat of the sun. She was kneeling on the blanket, sitting on her heels, aware of him with a fine-tuned radar.

"The food was very good. Thanks for the picnic, Eve." His hand reached out to cup the back of her head and pull her forward.

Lifting her gaze, she watched the sensual line of his mouth coming closer. She couldn't have resisted him if she wanted to, which she didn't. Her eyes closed an instant before his mouth touched her lips, then moved onto them to linger an instant. The kiss started her trembling all the way to her toes. Much too soon he was lifting his head, leaving her lips aching for the warm pressure of his mouth.

The very brevity of the kiss reminded her that it was a gesture of gratitude. It had meant no more than a peck on the cheek. She would be foolish to read more into it than that. Lowering her head, she struggled to appear unmoved by the experience, as casual about it as he seemed to be. Her fingers fastened on the wicker handle of the picnic basket.

"Do you want to put this in the boat now?" She picked it up to hand it to him, her gaze slanting upward.

For an instant Eve was subjected to the probing search of his narrowed eyes. Then his smooth smile erased the sensation as he took the picnic basket from her.

"Might as well," Luck agreed idly, and pushed to his feet.

Standing up, Eve resisted the impulse to

watch him walk to the boat. Instead she shook the crumbs and grains of sand off the blanket and folded it into a square. Feeling the isolation again, she turned her gaze to the treed interior of the island. The blanket was clutched in front of her, pressed protectively to her fluttering stomach. Behind her Eve heard the approach of Luck's footsteps in the sand.

"Where do you suppose Toby has gone?" she wondered.

"Leave the blanket here. We'll see if we can find him," Luck suggested, and took her hand after she'd laid the blanket down.

His easy possession sent a warm thrill over her skin. Eve liked the sensation of her slender hand being lost in the largeness of his. Together they walked to the narrow trail Toby had taken, where they would have to proceed single file.

"I'll go first, in case we run into some briers. I wouldn't want your legs to be scratched up." The downward sweep of his gaze took note of the bareness of her legs below the white shorts.

Instead of releasing her hand to start up the path, as Eve had expected he would, Luck curved his arm behind his back and shifted his grip to lead her. The forest shadows swallowed them up, the ground spongy beneath the faintly marked earth, the smell of pine resin heavy in the air.

Out of sight of their picnic site, a fallen timber blocked the trail, its huge trunk denoting the forest giant it had once been. Luck released her hand to climb over it and waited on the other side to help her. The rubber sole of her shoe found a foothold on the broken nub of a limb, providing her a step to the top of the trunk. All around them was dense foliage, with only a vague glitter of the lake's surface shining through the leaves.

"I'm glad this is a small island," Eve remarked. "A person could get lost in this."

"It's practically a jungle," Luck agreed.

His hands gripped the curves of her waist, spanning her hipbones to help her down. Eve steadied herself by placing her hands on his shoulders while he lifted her off the trunk to the ground. When it was solidly beneath her, she discovered the toes of her shoes were touching his, a hand's length separating them.

Beneath her hands she felt his flexed muscles go taut, his hands retaining their hold on her waist. Looking up, Eve saw his keen gaze going over every facet of her appearance. She became conscious of the lack of lipstick and the wind-ratted hair. It caused a tension that forced her to speak so it would be broken.

"I should have brought a comb. My hair is a mess," she remarked tightly.

Luck's gaze wandered slowly over it and back to her face, the color of his eyes changing, deepening. "It looks like a man mussed it while he was making love to you."

His hand reached to smooth the hair away from her face and cup the back of her head. The idle caress parted Eve's lips in a silent breath, fastening his attention on them. While his mouth began moving inexorably closer, his other hand shifted to her lower spine and applied pressure to gather her in.

The tension flowed out of her with a piercing sweetness as his mouth finally reached its destination. It rocked slowly over her lips, tasting and testing first this curve, then another. The trip-hammer beat of her heart revealed the havoc he was raising with her senses.

This intimate investigation didn't stop there. His hard warm lips continued their foray, grazing over her cheek to the sensitive area around her ear. Growing weaker, her hands inched to his shoulders, clinging to him for support and balance in this dizzying embrace.

"Do you have any idea how good this feels, Eve?" he murmured in a rough disturbed tone.

She felt the shuddering breath he took and moaned softly in an aching reply. It turned his head, bringing it to a different angle as he took firm possession of her lips, the territory already familiar to him from the last exploration. Now Luck staked his claim to it and made a driving search into the dark recesses of her mouth.

Eve curved her arms around his neck, seeking the springing thickness of his hair. His hands began roaming restlessly over her shoulders and back, left bare by the red halter top she wore. The softness of her curves were pressed and shaped to his hard bone and taut muscle. The kiss deepened until Eve was raw with the hot ache that burned within her.

Gradually she felt the passion withdrawing from his kiss. It ended before his mouth reluctantly ended the contact. Breathless and dazed, she slowly lowered her chin until it was level. She was conscious that Luck was trying to force his lungs to breathe normally. She tried to get a hold of her own emotions, but without his success. His head continued to be bent toward her, his chin and mouth at a level with her eyes.

"We'll never find Toby this way," he said finally.

"No, we won't," Eve agreed, and self-consciously brought her hands down from around his neck.

He loosened his hold, stepping back to create room between them. She slid a glance at him, trying to obtain a clue as to how she was expected to treat this kiss. Luck was half-turned, looking down the trail. Something was troubling his expression, but it smoothed into a smile when he glanced at her. Yet Eve was conscious that a faint puzzled light shaded his eyes.

"Toby can't be far. The island is too small," he said, and reached for her hand again before starting up the trail.

Twenty yards farther, they reached the opposite shore of the island and found Toby sitting on a waterlogged stump at the lake's edge. He hopped down when he saw them.

"Are we ready to go?" he asked with an unconcern that didn't match the bright curiosity of his eyes.

"If you are," Luck replied.

Toby's presence brought back the easygoing friendly atmosphere that had marked the beginning of the excursion. Not once did Eve feel uncomfortable, yet an uncertainty stayed with her. She couldn't tell whether Luck regarded her as a woman or a friend.

He beached the boat on the shore in front of her parents' cottage and gave her a hand to dry land. There was nothing in his manner to indicate he would accept an invitation to come to the house for a drink, so Eve didn't issue one.

"I enjoyed myself," she said instead. "Thanks for asking me to come along."

"It was our pleasure. Maybe we'll do it again sometime." It was a noncommittal reply, indefinite, promising nothing.

Eve tried not to let her disappointment show as she clutched the picnic basket and the blouse she hadn't worn. After waving goodbye to Toby aboard the boat, she struck out for the road and the log cottage opposite it.

SINCE HE'D LEFT EVE, the frown around his forehead and eyes had deepened. As he walked the path from the lake to his house, Luck tried to recall the last time he'd felt as alive as he had those few brief moments when he'd held Eve and kissed her. The deadness inside him had gone. He worried at it, searching for it in some hidden corner, barely conscious of Toby ambling along behind him.

"Dad?" Toby requested his attention and received an abstract glance. "Why do people kiss?"

That brought Luck sharply out of his reverie. He shortened his strides to let Toby catch up with him and raised a suspicious eyebrow. "Because they like each other." He gave a general answer.

Toby turned his head to eye him thoughtfully. "Have you ever kissed anybody you didn't like?"

Luck knew it was a loaded question, but he answered it anyway. "No."

"If you only kiss people you like, then you must like Eve," Toby concluded. The sharply questioning look couldn't be ignored, and the boy admitted, "I saw you and Eve. I was coming back to see if you were ready to leave, but you were so busy kissing her that you didn't hear me."

"No, I didn't hear you," Luck admitted grimly. The hot rush of emotion had deafened him to everything but the soft sounds of submission she made. He was bothered by a vague sense of infidelity. "And, yes, I like Eve."

"Why don't you marry her?"

"Liking isn't loving." Luck cast an irritated glance at his son. "And I thought it was understood that that subject was closed."

There was a long sigh from Toby but no comment.

LATER THAT NIGHT Toby was sprawled on the floor of the living room, arms crossed on a throw pillow, his chin resting in the hollow of his fists while he watched television. At a commercial, he turned to glance at his father in the easy chair—only he wasn't there.

Frowning, Toby pushed up on his hands to peer into the kitchen, but there was no sign of him. His father hadn't been acting right since the boat ride. That fact prompted Toby to go in search of him.

He found him in a darkened bedroom. The hallway light spilled in to show him sitting on the bed, elbows on his knees and his chin resting on clasped hands. Toby paused in the doorway for a minute, confused until he saw that his father was staring at the framed photograph of his mother on the dresser.

Toby walked up to him and laid a comforting hand on his shoulder. "What's wrong, dad?"

Bringing his hands down, Luck turned his head, paused, then sighed heavily. A smile broke half-heartedly. "Nothing, sport."

But Toby glanced at the picture. "Were you thinking about mom?"

There was a wry twist to his father's mouth. "No, I wasn't." Pushing to his feet, he rested a hand on Toby's shoulder. Together they left the room. As they walked out the door, Toby stole a glance over his shoulder at the picture of the smiling tawny-haired blonde. He slipped his small hand into his father's, but he knew it was small comfort.

THE NEXT DAY Toby's stomach insisted it was lunchtime. Entering the house through the back door, he walked into the kitchen. His arrival coincided with his father saying a final goodbye to an unknown party on the telephone extension in the kitchen.

"I'll tell him. Right...I'll be there," Luck said, and hung up.

His curiosity overflowed, as it usually did. "Who was that? Tell me what? Where will you be?" The questions tumbled out with barely a breath in between.

"Your granddad said hello," Luck replied, answering two questions.

"Why didn't you let me talk to him?" Toby frowned in disappointment.

"Because he was busy. Next time, okay?" his father promised, and glanced at the wall clock. "I suppose you want lunch. What will it be? Hamburgers? Grilled cheese? How about some soup?"

"Hamburgers," Toby chose without a great

deal of interest or enthusiasm. Hooking an arm around a chair back, he watched his father take the meat from the refrigerator and carry it to the stove, where he shaped portions into patties to put in the skillet. "You said you'd be there. Be where? When?"

"I have to drive to Duluth this Friday to meet with your grandfather," Luck replied, and half turned to instruct, "Put the ketchup and mustard on the table."

"I suppose you're going to ask Mrs. Jackson to come over to stay with me," Toby grumbled as he went about setting the table and putting on the condiments.

"You are absolutely right. I'm calling her after lunch."

"Oh, dad, do you have to?" Toby appealed to him. "Sometimes Mrs. Jackson is a real pain."

"Has it ever occurred to you that Mrs. Jackson might think you are a real pain?" his father countered.

"She always thinks I'm making up stories."

"I wonder why?" Luck murmured dryly.

Toby let the silverware clatter to the table as a thought occurred to hm. "Why couldn't you ask Eve to come over? If I *have* to have somebody sit with me, I'd rather it was Eve."

Luck hesitated, and Toby studied that momentary indecision with interest. "I'll ask her," his father finally agreed.

"You'll call her after lunch?" Toby persisted for a more definite agreement.

"Yes."

EVE WAS HALFWAY OUT THE DOOR with her arms full of suntan lotion, blanket and a paperback for an afternoon in the sun when the telephone rang. She ended up dropping everything but the lotion onto couch cushions before she got the receiver to her ear.

"Rowlands," she answered.

"Hello, Eve?" Luck's voice responded on the other end of the line.

She tossed the suntan lotion on top of the blanket and hugged her free arm around her middle, holding tight to the pleasure of his voice. "Yes, this is Eve."

"Luck McClure," he needlessly identified himself. "Are you busy this Friday?"

"No." She and her mother had tentatively talked about a shopping expedition into Cable, but that certainly could be postponed.

"I have a large favor to ask. I have some business· I have to take care of on Friday, which means I'll be gone most of the day and late into the evening. Toby asked if you would stay with him while I'm gone instead of the woman who usually sits with him."

Swallowing her disappointment, Eve smoothly agreed, "I don't mind in the least looking after Toby. What time would you like me to come?"

"I'd like to get an early start. Would eight o'clock be too early?" Luck asked.

"I can be there by eight."

"Thanks. Toby will be glad to know you're coming," he said. "We'll see you on Friday."

"On Friday," Eve repeated, and echoed his goodbye.

Toby would be glad she was coming, he'd said. Did that mean that Luck wouldn't? Eve sighed wearily because she simply didn't know.

ON FRIDAY morning her father dropped her off at the lake house a few minutes before eight. As she got out of the car, he leaned over to remind her, "If you need anything, you be sure to call us. Your mother or I can be over in a matter of minutes."

"I will. Thanks, dad." She waved to him and hurried toward the house.

Toby had obviously been watching for her because the front door opened before she reached it. He stood in the opening, a broad smile of welcome on his face.

"Hi, Eve."

"Hello, Toby." Her gaze went past him to the tall figure approaching the door as she entered.

The fluttering of her pulse signaled the heightening of her senses. Eve had never seen Luck in business clothes, and the dark suit and tie altered his appearance in a way that intensified the aura of male authority, dominating and powerful.

"Right on time." He smiled in an absent fashion. "I left a phone number by the telephone. You can reach me there if you have an emergency."

"Which I hope I won't," she replied, trying to respond with her usual naturalness.

After a glance of agreement, he laid a hand on Toby's head. "Behave yourself. Otherwise Eve will make you stand in a corner."

"No, she won't." Toby dipped his head to avoid the mussing of his father's hand.

His smile held a trace of affection and indulgence toward his son when Luck turned to Eve. "I shouldn't be too late getting back tonight."

"Don't worry about it," she assured him. "Toby and I will be all right."

"You know how to reach me if you need me," Luck reminded her, and she tried not to be disappointed because the remark held no underlying meaning. It was a straightforward statement from a father to a sitter. "I have to be going," he addressed both of them and smiled at his son. "See you later."

"Tell granddad hi for me," Toby instructed.

"I will," Luck promised.

To get out the door, Luck had to walk past Eve. His arm inadvertently brushed against hers, sending a little quiver through her limbs. When she breathed in, she caught the musky scent of his male after-shave lotion, potently stimulating as the man who wore it. The essence of him seemed to linger even afer he'd walked out the door.

With Toby standing beside her on the threshold, Eve watched him walk to the car. She returned his wave when he reversed out of the driveway onto the road and felt a definite sensation of being part of the family—standing at the doorway with her "son" and waving goodbye to her "husband."

Eve shook the thought away. It was that kind of dangerous thinking that would lead to heartbreak. It was definitely not wise. She was a baby-sitter—that's all.

Fixing a bright smile on her mouth, she looked down at Toby. "What's on the agenda this morning?"

He shrugged and tipped his head back to give her a bright-eyed look that reminded her a lot of his father. "I don't know. Do you want to play catch?"

"Do you think we'll break a window?" Eve teased.

"I hope not," Toby declared with a grim look. "I had to spend half the money I was saving for a minibike to pay my share of the damage to your windshield. Dad paid for most of it 'cause it was mostly his fault for throwing the ball too high, but he wouldn't have been playing if it hadn't been for me. We share things."

"Yes, I can see that," she nodded, because the two seemed to have a remarkable relationship, unique to anything she'd come across in her meetings with parents at school.

"Do you want to play catch?" he repeated his suggestion.

"Sure," Eve agreed, even though she didn't feel obligated to entertain him. The idea of being active appealed to her. "Go get your ball and glove."

"I'll bring dad's for you," he offered. "Sometimes I throw it pretty hard—" Toby warned "—and it stings your hand when you catch it."

The driveway seemed the safest place to play catch since there weren't any windows in the line of fire. When Toby tired of that, they walked down by the lake, where he gave her lessons in the fine art of skipping stones on the lake's surface.

At noon they returned to the lake cabin. "What would you like for lunch?" Eve asked as they entered through the kitchen door.

"A peanut butter sandwich and a glass of milk is okay." He didn't sound enthused by his own suggestion.

"Is that what you usually have?" she asked.

"It's easy," Toby shrugged. "Dad and I aren't much for cooking."

"How about if I check the refrigerator and see if there's anything else to eat?" Eve suggested, certain that Toby would like something more imaginative if she offered to fix it.

"Go ahead," he agreed, then warned, "There's not-much in there except some frozen dinners in the freezer section of the icebox."

When she opened the refrigerator door, she discovered Toby was right. The shelves were nearly bare, except for milk, eggs, bacon and a couple of jars of jam.

Toby watched her expression. "I told you," he reminded her. "Dad fixes breakfast and sometimes cooks steaks on the grill. Otherwise we eat out or have frozen dinners. They're pretty good, though."

Eve found a package of cheese in the dairy drawer of the refrigerator. "Do you like grilled cheese sandwiches?" she asked.

"Yeah," he nodded.

While the skillet was heating to grill them, Eve searched through the cupboards and found a lone can of condensed tomato soup. She diluted it with milk and added a dab of butter. When she set the lunch on the table, Toby consumed it with all the gusto of the growing boy that he was.

"Boy, that was good, Eve!" he declared, and leaned back in his chair to rub his full stomach. "You sure are a good cook."

"Grilling a sandwich and opening a can of soup isn't exactly cooking," she smiled. "I was thinking that I might call my father and see if he would drive us to the store this afternoon and pick up some groceries. I'll cook you a *real* dinner tonight. Would you like that?''

"You bet!''

CHAPTER SIX

AFTER A FEW INQUIRIES Eve was able to discover some of Toby's favorite dishes. Being a young boy, he had simple tastes. Dinner that evening consisted of fried chicken, mashed potatoes and gravy and some early sweet corn-on-the-cob. For dessert she fixed fresh strawberry shortcake with lots of whipped cream.

"I can't ever remember eating food that good," Toby insisted. "It was really delicious, Eve."

"Why, thank you, sir." With her hands full of dirty dishes to be carried to the sink, she gave him a mock curtsy.

"I'll help wash the dishes," he volunteered, and pushed away from the table. "Dad usually dries them."

"You don't need to help." She had already learned while she was preparing the meal that Toby was accustomed to doing household chores. His sense of duty was commendable, but he was still very young and needed a break from it once in a while. "You can have the night off and I'll do them."

"Really?" He seemed stunned by her offer.

"Yes, really," she laughed.

"I'll stay and keep you company." He dragged a chair over to the kitchen counter by the sink.

"I'd like that," Eve said, and let the sink fill with water, squirting liquid soap into it.

Kneeling on the chair seat, Toby rested his arms on the counter and propped his chin on an upraised hand to watch her. "You know, it'd really be great to have a mother. It's getting to be a hassle cleaning the house, washing dishes and all that stuff."

"I can imagine." She smiled faintly as she began washing the dishes and rinsing them under the running faucet, then setting them on the draining board to dry.

"I'd sure like to figure out how to find someone for dad to marry." Toby sighed his frustration. "I thought about putting an ad in the paper, but dad really got upset when I mentioned it to him."

Her initial pang of envy came from the knowledge that she coveted the role of Toby's mother—and Luck's wife. It wouldn't take much encouragement to fall head over heels in love with Luck. She was already more than halfway there now.

But after the brief envy came amusement and sympathy for Luck's plight. The idea of advertising for a wife had to have come as a shock to him.

"It would have been a little embarrassing for your father, Toby," Eve murmured, the corners of her mouth deepening with the smile she tried to contain.

"Dad seemed to think that, too." He grimaced in resignation to the decision. "I told dad that you'd make a good mother and he should marry you."

"Toby, you didn't!" She nearly dropped the dish in her hand, a warm pink flooding her cheeks.

"Yes, I did," he assured her innocently. "What's wrong with that? He likes you. I know he does. I saw him kiss you."

Eve became very busy with the dishes, trying to hide her agitation and embarrassment with her work. "Just because you kiss someone doesn't necessarily mean you want to marry them, Toby."

"Yeah, that's what dad said," he admitted.

She hated the curiosity that made her ask, "What else did your dad say when you suggested he should marry me?"

"Nothing. He told me the subject was closed and I wasn't supposed to discuss it anymore, but we need someone around here to take care of us." The comment revealed he hadn't let go of the idea. "There's too much work for a boy like me to do, and dad's busy. Somewhere there's a girl that dad will marry. I just gotta find her."

"Toby McClure, I think you should leave that to your father," Eve suggested.

"Yeah, but he isn't *trying* to find anybody," Toby protested. "I thought I'd have better luck." Then he laughed. "I made a joke, didn't I? Better luck for Luck."

"Yes, you did." Her smile widened into a grin.

"That's my name, too, you know," he declared, and settled his chin on his hand once more.

"No, I didn't know that." Her brown eyes widened in vague surprise. "I thought it was Toby—Tobias," she corrected it from the shortened version.

"That's my middle name," Toby explained. "My real first name is Luck—like my dad's. My mom insisted on naming me after him when I was born, but dad said it was too hard growing up with a name like that. He said I'd wind up getting called Little Luck, and he didn't like the idea of being Big Luck. So they called me Toby instead."

"I think that was probably best," Eve agreed with the decision.

In her experience at the school, she'd seen how cruel children could be sometimes when one of the members had an unusual name. Sometimes they teased him unmercifully. As a rule children didn't like being different. It wasn't until later, when their sense of individuality surfaced, that they showed a desire for unique names.

Yet she couldn't help remembering when she had first been introduced to the father and son, and Luck had explained the family tradition of his name. At the time she had wondered if there was a "little" Luck at home to carry it on. It was slightly amusing to discover it had been Toby all along.

After the dishes were done, she and Toby went into the front room and watched television for a while. At nine o'clock she suggested that it was time he took a bath and got ready for bed. He didn't argue or try to persuade her to let him stay up until Luck came home.

Spanking clean from his bath, Toby trotted barefoot into the living room in his pajamas. He half flopped himself across the armrest of the chair where Eve was sitting.

"Are you going to tuck me into bed?" he asked.

"I sure am." Eve smiled at the irresistible appeal of his look. Toby was just as capable of twisting her around his finger as his roguish father was.

Toby led the way to his room while Eve followed. He made a running leap at the bed, dived under the covers and was settled comfortably by the time Eve arrived at his bedside. A white pillowcase framed the mass of dark brown hair as a pair of bright blue eyes looked back at her.

She made a show of tucking the covers close to his sides while he kept his arms on top of them. Then she sat sideways on the edge of the mattress.

"You don't have to read me a story or anything," Toby said. "I'm too old for that."

"Okay. Would you like me to leave the light on for a while?" Eve asked, referring to the small lamp burning on the bedside table. She already suspected he was "too old" for that, too.

"No." There was a negative movement of his head against the pillow.

Her glance had already been drawn to the night table, where it was caught by the framed photograph of a beautiful blond-haired woman with sparkling green eyes. A vague pain splintered through Eve as she guessed the identity of the smiling face in the photograph.

"Is this a picture of your mother?" she asked Toby for confirmation, her throat hurting.

"Yes. Her name was Lisa." Toby blithely passed on the information.

"She's very beautiful," Eve admitted, aware that Luck would never have called this woman a "brown mouse." She was golden—all sunshine and springtime. Eve despised herself for the jealousy that was twisting inside her. But she didn't have a prayer of ever competing with someone as beautiful as this girl—not even with her memory. It was utterly hopeless to think Luck would ever love her.

"Dad has a picture just like that in his room," Toby informed her. "He talks to it a lot...although he hasn't lately," he added as an afterthought.

"I'm sure he loves her very much." She tried to smile and conceal the awful aching inside. "It's time you were going to sleep."

"Will you kiss me good-night?" he asked with an unblinking look.

"Of course." There was a tightness in her throat as Eve bent toward him and brushed his forehead with a kiss. She longed for the right to do that every night. She straightened, murmuring, "Have a nice night, Toby."

"Good night, Eve." With a contented look on his face, he snuggled deeper under the covers.

Her hand faltered as she reached past the framed photograph to turn out the light. Standing up, she moved silently out of the room. Bitter tears burned the back of her eyes. She regretted more than she ever had in her life that she had been born plain.

In the living room Eve turned down the volume on the television set and picked up a magazine lying on the coffee table. Curling up in the large armchair, she tried to force herself to read the articles it contained. The clock on the fireplace mantel ticked away the time.

IT WAS AFTER MIDNIGHT when Luck pulled into the driveway, much later than he had anticipated. Switching off the engine, he grabbed his briefcase and his suit jacket from the rear seat. The briefcase he carried in his hand as he climbed out of the car; the jacket he swung over his shoulder, held by the hook of a finger. His tie was draped loosely around his neck, the top buttons of his shirt unfastened.

The tension of a long drive and the mental fatigue from a full day of business discussions cramped the muscles in his shoulders and neck. Weariness drew tired lines in his tough rakehell features.

As Luck walked to the front door of the cabin, he noticed the light burning in the window. The edges of his mouth lifted in a faint smile at the welcoming sight. When he opened the door, he heard the muted volume of the television set. There was a warm run of pleasure as he realized Eve must have waited up for him to come home.

Setting his briefcase down just inside the door, he walked into the living room and paused. Eve had fallen asleep in the big armchair, with a magazine in her lap. His smile lengthened at the sight of her curled up like a velvety brown mouse. Luck tossed his suit jacket onto the sofa along with his tie and walked over to turn off the television set.

Silence swirled through the room as he approached the chair where she was sleeping. He intended to wake her, but when he looked down at her, the tiredness seemed to fall away from him. In repose, her serene features reminded him of the gentle beauty of a madonna—or a sleeping beauty waiting to be wakened with a kiss. The latter was a tantalizing thought.

Leaning down, Luck placed his hands on either armrest of the armchair. He felt alive and whole, renewed by her presence. He lowered his mouth onto her lips, stimulated by their sweet softness. At the initial contact, they were unresponsive to the mobile pressure of his kiss. Then Luck felt her lips move against his. Raw emotions surged through him, an aching pressure building inside him.

Eve stirred with the beginnings of wakefulness and he pulled back, not straightening but continuing to lean over her. The desire was strong to pick her up and carry her into his bedroom where he could give rein to those feelings that swept him.

Her lashes slowly drifted open and he watched the dawning light of recognition flare in her brown, nearly black eyes. His blood was warmed by the pleasure at seeing him that ran wild in her look.

"You're home," she murmured in soft joy.

"Yes," Luck answered huskily, because it seemed he had come home. It was a sensation he couldn't quite explain, not even to himself.

One minute he could see the welcome in her eyes and in the next it was gone, as a sudden rush of self-consciousness hid it from him. She lowered her chin, a vague agitation making her restive.

"I must have fallen asleep." She brushed a hand across her eyes, then reached for the opened magazine in her lap.

Faintly irritated by her sudden remoteness, Luck pushed himself erect, withdrawing physically from her as she had withdrawn from him. He saw the flicker of her hurt in the velvet darkness of her eyes. Luck regretted the day he'd ever called her a brown mouse. Her sensitive nature had found the phrase offensive when he had actually used it with teasing affection.

All Eve knew about what he was feeling she saw in the displeasure written on his features. There was a vague sensation that he had kissed her, but she thought she had dreamed that.

"What time is it?" There was a crick in her neck from sleeping in the chair. She rubbed at the stiffness as she uncurled her legs.

"It's nearly one." His answer was abrupt. "I'm sorry I was so late getting back."

"It's all right." Eve smiled in his direction without actually meeting his gaze.

"You didn't have to wait up for me." It almost sounded like a criticism. "You should have lain down on the couch."

"I didn't plan to fall asleep. I was reading and...I guess I dozed off," she explained self-consciously.

"Let me check on Toby, then I'll drive you home," he said.

Luck disappeared into the darkened hallway leading to the bedrooms as Eve forced her cramped body out of the chair. She noticed his suit jacket and tie on the sofa when she retrieved her purse from the coffee table. She remembered how incredibly handsome he'd looked when she'd opened her eyes and seen him standing there, bent over her to wake her. He must have seen the rush of love she'd felt. There didn't seem to be any other explanation for the way he'd withdrawn from her—his sudden shortness. He probably thought she was going to start fawning all over him and didn't want the embarrassment of her unwanted attentions. She resolved not to let him see the way she felt toward him, not again.

When he returned to the living room, Eve managed to appear very calm and controlled—and very casual. Yet there wasn't any approval in his inspecting glance.

"Ready?" he asked.

"Yes." She had to look away from him before she was affected by his blatant masculinity. "Is Toby all right?"

"He's sound asleep," Luck replied. "He'll be okay alone until I get back."

"Of course," she murmured, and moved toward the front door.

Outside, a full moon bathed the night with its

silvery light and the sky was atwinkle with stars. A breeze whispered through the pines, scenting the air with their freshness. Eve paused beside the passenger side of the car while Luck opened the door for her.

Nervousness made her say, "It's a lovely evening, isn't it?" The ambience seemed too romantic for her peace of mind.

"Yes, it is," Luck agreed, and waited until she was inside before closing the door.

Her gaze followed him as he walked around the car and slid behind the wheel. When he started the motor, Eve faced the front. Her nerve ends quivered with his nearness, making the silence intolerable.

"How did your business go today?" she asked, to make conversation.

"Fine." It was a noncommunicative answer, but Luck made it easier by asking, "Did Toby give you any trouble today?"

"None," Eve assured him. At this time of night there was no traffic on the road to her parents' lake cottage. They had it all to themselves. "We played catch—and didn't break a single window," she added with feigned lightness.

"You're luckier than I am." He slid her a brief glance, one side of his mouth lifting in a half smile, his voice dry with amusement.

"We were careful about the area we picked," she explained, relaxing a little under the humorous overtones of the subject matter.

It was a short drive to the cottage. Part of her regretted the quickness with which they covered the distance, and another part of her was relieved. When they drove in, Eve noticed her parents had left the porch light burning.

"I hope they weren't worried about you," Luck commented as he stopped the car.

"I doubt it," she replied. "They've accepted that I'm a big girl now. My hours are my own."

Letting the engine idle, he shifted the gear into the park and half turned in the seat to face her. "How much do I owe you for staying with Toby?"

She stiffened at the offer of payment for her services. "Nothing," Eve insisted.

"I didn't ask you to stay with Toby with the intentions of getting a free baby-sitter. If you hadn't come, I would have had to pay someone else," Luck reasoned.

"Please don't ask me to take money for this," she appealed to him, not wanting to be paid for something she had done gladly. "Just consider it a favor from a neighbor."

"All right." He gave in reluctantly. "I won't argue with you."

"Thank you." Eve looked away to reach for the door handle, but she was kept from opening it by the staying hand that touched her arm.

Almost against her will, she looked back at him. The sheen of the moonlight bronzed the masculine angles and planes of his face, giving them a rugged look. A hunger rose within her that she couldn't deny.

"Thank you for staying with Toby." His voice was pitched disturbingly low, vibrant in its rich tone.

"You're welcome," Eve whispered the reply, too affected by his touch and his nearness to speak normally.

Nor could she draw away when his head bent toward hers. She trembled under the possession of his hard lips, her resolve shattering into a thousand pieces. His hand spanned her rib cage just below the uplift of her breast and silently urged her closer.

Eve arched nearer, trying to satisfy the hunger she tasted in his kiss. The blood pounded in her ears with a thunderous force as she let him part her lips to savor the completeness of her response. A soft moan came from her throat at the ache Luck aroused in her.

He was everything. Her senses were dominated by him. The feel of his rock-hard muscles excited her hesitant hands, which rested lightly on his chest, warmed by the heat generated from his male body. That combination of scents—tobacco smoke, musky cologne and his own male scent—filled her lungs with its heady mixture. And the taste of him was in her mouth.

The world was spinning crazily, but Eve didn't care—as long as she had him to cling to. Kissing him was both heaven and hell. But regardless of the consequences, she seemed to be condemned to loving him.

Luck dragged his mouth from her lips and let it moistly graze over her cheek, trailing fire Her breath was so shallow, it was practically nonexistent. He combed his fingers into her hair as if to hold her head still.

"And thanks for waiting up for me, Eve," he murmured thickly against her sensitive skin. "It's been a long time since anyone has done that. I can't explain how good it made me feel."

"Luck, I. . . ." But she was afraid to say the words. Then he kissed her again and she didn't need to say anything.

But this time it was brief, although she had the consolation of sensing his reluctance when it ended and he drew away.

"I've got to get back. Toby's alone," Luck said, as if he needed to explain.

"Yes." This time he made no move to stop her when she opened the door. "Good night," she murmured as she stepped out of the car.

"Good night, Eve," he responded.

She seemed to glide on air to the lighted porch, conscious that Luck was waiting to make sure she got safely inside. Opening the door, she turned and waved to him. She watched the red taillights of his car until they disappeared onto the road.

It would be so easy to read something significant into his kisses. Eve tried desperately to guard against raising false hopes. Thinking about the photograph of his late wife helped. That, and the memory of the time when he had intimated he was lonely.

As she undressed for bed, Eve berated herself for being such a fool as to let herself love him. It was very difficult to listen when she felt so good.

THIS TIME there were no lights burning to welcome him home when Luck entered the cabin. He didn't bother to turn any on as he made his way down the hallway in the dark.

"Dad?" Toby's sleepy voice called out to him.

"Yes, son, it's me." He paused by the doorway to his son's room.

"Did you take Eve home?" Toby asked.

"Yes. I just got back," he explained. "Are you okay?"

"Yeah." There was the rustle of bedcovers shifting. "How was granddad?"

"He's fine," Luck assured him. "It's very late. You go back to sleep, Toby. We'll talk in the morning."

"Okay, dad," he replied in the middle of a yawn. "Good night."

"Good night, Toby." Luck waited until he heard silence from the room, then entered his own.

The moonlight shining in through the window

illuminated the room sufficiently, allowing him to undress without the need of turning on the bed lamp. Unbuttoning his shirt, he pulled it free from the waistband of his pants and shrugged out of it to toss it into the clothes hamper.

He sat down on the edge of the bed to take off his shoes. The moon laid its light on the framed photograph sitting on his dresser. Luck stopped to gaze at it.

"We had a good thing, Lisa," he murmured. "But it was a long time ago." There was an amused lift to his mouth, a little on the wry side. "Why do I have the feeling that you don't mind if I fall in love with someone else?"

But she didn't answer him. It had been quite a while since she had. Luck wasn't haunted anymore by images from the past. And he didn't feel any guilt that it was so.

CHAPTER SEVEN

THE AFTERNOON SUN burned into her oiled skin as Eve shifted her position in the reclining lounge chair. Dark sunglasses blocked out most of the glare, but the scarlet swimsuit exposed her body to the sun's tanning rays. The straps were unfastened so that they wouldn't leave any white strips on her shoulders.

When she reached for her glass of iced tea sitting under the chair in the shade, Eve held the bodice in position with her hand so that the top wouldn't fall down when she bent over. The sip of tea momentarily cooled and refreshed her. She'd promised herself to walk down to the lake for a swim, but so far she hadn't found the energy.

The front screen door creaked on its hinges and Eve turned her head toward the lake cottage as her mother stepped onto the porch. She saw Eve and smiled.

"There you are," she declared. "I was ready to hike down to the lake. You're wanted on the telephone."

"Me?" She almost forgot about the untied

straps of her swimsuit as she sat up abruptly. A quicksilver run of excitement sped through her nerves. "Who is it?"

"It's Luck McClure," her mother answered.

"Tell him I'll be right there," Eve urged.

Her fingers turned into thumbs as she tried hurriedly to knot the straps behind her neck. While she struggled with that, the leather thongs refused to cooperate with her attempts to slip her bare feet into them. She heard the screen door swing shut behind her mother.

The message was being passed to Luck that she was on her way to the phone, but Eve was afraid he'd get tired of waiting if she took too long. When she finally had the straps tied and the shoes on, she ran to the cottage.

The telephone receiver was off the hook, lying beside the phone on the table. Eve grabbed it up, mindless of the amused glances exchanged by her parents.

"Hello?" She was winded from her panicked rush to the phone—and the breathless excitement she couldn't control.

"Eve? You sound out of breath," Luck's voice observed, and she closed her eyes in silent relief that he hadn't hung up.

"I was outside." She swallowed in an attempt to steady her breathing.

"Your mother told me that she thought you were down by the lake," he admitted.

"Actually, I wasn't," Eve explained. "I was out front, sunbathing."

"Wearing a skimpy little bikini, I suppose," Luck murmured.

"No." She half smiled. "I have on a very respectable one-piece bathing suit."

"I should have guessed." His voice was dry with contained amusement.

The reply stung her sensitive ego. She knew exactly what he was thinking. A one-piece suit was precisely what a brown mouse would wear. After all, they weren't very daring creatures.

"Why are you calling, Luck?" She supposed he wanted her to stay with Toby again. It was really quite a bargain when baby-sitters could be paid with a kiss. After last night what else could he think?

"I called to ask you to have dinner with us tonight. Since you wouldn't let me pay you anything for staying with Toby, I thought you might accept an invitation to dinner," he explained.

If he hadn't added the explanation, she would probably have leaped at the invitation, but he stole the pleasure from it.

"I told you last night that I was just being a friendly neighbor," Eve reminded him stiffly. "I don't expect anything in return. And you certainly aren't obligated to take me to dinner."

"I'm not asking out of any sense of duty,"

Luck stated on a note of tolerance. "Toby and I *want* you to come over for dinner tonight."

"Thank you, but I—" She started to refuse politely for her pride's sake, but he interrupted her.

"Before you turn me down, you'd better hear the terms of the invitation." A faint thread of amusement ran through his voice.

"Terms?" Eve repeated with a bewildered frown.

"Ever since Toby got up this morning, he's been bragging about what a great cook you are," he informed her. "It's been a long time since I've had a home-cooked meal, so I decided to ask you over to dinner tonight and find out if Toby knows what he's talking about."

She was a little stunned by the implication of his reply, and faintly amused. "Do you mean you're asking me to dinner and you're expecting me to cook it?"

"Only part of it," Luck assured her. "I've got some steaks, so I'll take care of the meat course. The rest of the menu I'll leave to you."

"You have a lot of nerve, Luck McClure." But she couldn't help laughing.

"What do you say?" he challenged. "Is it a deal? Will you come tonight?"

"What time?" she asked, and smiled at the mouthpiece of the receiver.

"I'll pick you up at six o'clock. Is that all right?" he asked.

"That's fine," Eve nodded. "I'll be ready."

"I'll see you at six," Luck promised, and rang off.

Her smile lingered as she replaced the receiver on its cradle and turned away from the phone. She happened to glance at her father and caught the merry twinkle in his hazel eyes.

"I take it that you're going out to dinner with Luck," he guessed from the one side of the conversation he'd heard. "You've been seeing quite a bit of him lately. Maybe I should have a chat with him when he comes to pick you up tonight and find out his intentions."

He was only teasing, but Eve reacted just the same. "Don't you dare," she warned, and he laughed.

AS PART OF HER NEW IMAGE to rid herself of the brown-mouse label, Eve wore a white blouse of eyelet lace that scalloped to a vee neckline and buttoned down the front. With it she wore a pair of cornflower-blue slacks in a clingy material.

Promptly at six o'clock, Luck drove up to the cottage, accompanied by Toby. Ready and waiting, Eve bolted from the cabin before her father had a chance to tease her further by carrying out his threat to "have a little talk" with Luck.

Toby whistled like an adult wolf when he saw her. Eve flushed a little. She hadn't thought the different style and color of clothes made that much difference in her appearance—enough for an eight-year-old to notice.

When Toby hopped into the rear seat so Eve could sit in front beside Luck, she was subjected to a wickedly admiring rake of his blue eyes. Her cheeks grew even warmer.

"Not bad," Luck murmured his approval.

Compliments from him were something she couldn't handle, so she tried to turn it aside with a self-effacing remark. "You mean, it's not bad for a brown mouse," Eve corrected.

"No, not a brown mouse anymore. A blue one," he declared with a glance at her slacks. After checking for traffic, Luck reversed onto the road.

"Did dad tell you we're going to have steaks tonight?" Toby leaned over the top of the front seat.

"Yes, he did," she admitted.

"How do you like yours cooked?" Luck asked.

"Medium rare." Her sensitive nerves felt just about that raw at the moment, ultraconscious of the man behind the wheel.

"I guessed you were the red-blooded kind." He allowed his gaze to leave the road long enough to send a mocking glance at her. The innuendo seemed to hint she had a passionate nature, which only served to heighten her awareness of him.

"That's the way we like ours, too, isn't it,

dad?'' Toby said, unconscious of any hidden meaning in the talk.

"It sure is," Luck agreed, a smile playing at the edges of his mouth.

"You have to watch him, though," Toby told Eve. "Or he winds up burning them."

"Now wait a minute," Luck said in protest. "Who's the cook around here?"

"Eve," his son was quick to answer.

A low chuckle came from Luck's throat. "That's a point well taken." He slowed the car as they approached the drive to the cabin.

Preparations for the evening meal became a family affair. Luck started the grill in the backyard and cooked the steaks, while Toby took care of setting the table and helping Eve. She fixed a fresh spinach salad and wild rice to go along with the steaks. There were enough strawberries left over from the previous night's shortcake dessert to add to other fruit for a mixed fruit sauce as a light dessert.

When they sat down at the table, the meal seemed flawless. Eve wasn't sure whether it was the food or the company that made it all taste so good, but all three of them ate every bite of food on their plates.

"Didn't I tell you Eve was a good cook?" Toby stayed at the table while they lingered over their coffee.

"You certainly did," Luck agreed. "And you were right, too."

"Your father deserves some of the credit," Eve insisted. "I don't know about yours, but my steak was perfect."

"Thank you." Luck inclined his dark head in mocking acceptance of the compliment. Thick strands of rich brown hair fell across his forehead, adding to his rakish air.

"Mine was good, too," Toby assured him, then took away the compliment. "But all you had to do was watch them so they wouldn't burn. Eve really did the cooking."

"And an excellent job, too." He didn't argue with his son's summation. The magnetic blue of his eyes centered on her, lazy and disturbing. "You certainly know the way to a man's heart."

All her senses went haywire at that remark, throwing her into a state of heady confusion. She struggled to conceal it, quickly dropping her gaze and busying her hands with the dessert dishes still on the table.

"Don't bother with the dishes," Luck instructed. "We'll just stack them in the sink for now."

"Nonsense." There was an agitated edge to her voice that betrayed her inner disturbance. "It will only take a few minutes to do them and they'll be out of the way."

"In that case, we'll all help." He pushed out of his chair. "You can clear the table and stack the dishes by the sink, and Toby can wash them while I dry.''

They seemed to get them done in record time. Eve finished wiping the stove, table and counter tops a little before Toby and Luck were through.

As the trio entered the living room, Toby turned to walk backward and face them. ''Why don't we start a fire in the fireplace, dad?''

''It's summer, Toby,'' Luck reminded him with an indulgent look.

''I know, but it would be fun,'' he shrugged. ''We could toast marshmallows.''

''You can't still be hungry,'' Eve laughed.

''No, but I'll eat them anyway,'' he replied, and she understood that most of the pleasure came from toasting them, rather than eating them. ''Please, dad. Just a little fire.''

''Okay,'' Luck gave in. ''Just a small one.''

While Toby dashed back to the kitchen for the bag of marshmallows and a long-handled toasting fork, Luck built a small fire in the stone fireplace. When it was burning nicely, the three of them sat on the floor in a semicircle around the hearth.

Toby did the actual toasting of the marsh-mallows, passing around the finished product in turns. Half a bag was consumed—mostly by the fire—before he finally tired of the task. All of them had to wash the sticky gooey residue from their hands. Once that was done, the flickering flames of a fading fire drew them back to their former positions.

A contented silence settled over the room, broken only by the soft crackle of the burning wood. Outside, darkness had descended and the soft glow of the fire provided the only light in the front room. Sitting cross-legged between them, Toby yawned loudly.

"Gosh, I'm tired," he declared. "I think I'll go to bed."

Luck wore a look of vague surprise that his son was actually volunteering to go to bed. A little thread of self-consciousness laced its way through Eve's nerve ends at the prospect of being alone with Luck.

"I guess it is your bedtime," Luck remarked as his son pushed to his feet with apparent tiredness.

"Yeah." Toby paused to look at Eve. "Thanks for cooking dinner tonight. It was really good."

"You're welcome." Her mouth trembled a little in its smile.

"Good night," he wished her.

"Good night," she returned.

"I'll be in shortly," Luck promised.

"You don't need to. You can stay with Eve," Toby said, then partially turned to hide the frowning look of reproval he gave his father from her. She heard him whisper, "I'm big enough to go to bed by myself. Don't embarrass me in front of her.''

A slow smile broke over Luck's features at his son's admonition. "Get to bed." He affectionately slapped Toby on the behind to send him on his way.

When he'd gone, Luck slid the lazy smile in Eve's direction, encompassing her with the warmth of its casual intimacy. There had been an ease between them. Eve had definitely felt it, yet without Toby's presence to serve as a buffer, it started to dissipate. She became conscious there was only the two of them in the room. The silence that had been so pleasant and comfortable began to grow heavy. She'd never had the knack for making idle conversation, but the situation seemed to demand it.

"He's quite the boy," Eve remarked under the strain of silence.

"Unfortunately he's grown old before his time." His smile twisted into a regretful grimace that held a certain resignation.

"I don't think he's suffered too much from it," she replied, because Toby did appear to have achieved a balance between his boyhood and his sense of responsibility.

"I guess he hasn't." Luck stared at the fire and seemed to lose himself in the tiny yellow flames darting their tongues over the glowing log.

Eve couldn't think of a response, and the silence lengthened. She supposed that he was thinking about his late wife, probably remembering past moments shared.

No more sounds came from the direction of Toby's bedroom, and the tension ran through her system. Her legs were becoming cramped by her curled sitting position, but Eve was reluctant to move and draw attention to herself. She didn't want Luck to look at her and mentally compare her to the beautiful blonde in the photograph.

At that moment he seemed to rouse himself and become aware that he wasn't alone. "That fire is becoming hypnotic," he said, explaining away his preoccupation.

"Yes." Eve pretended she had been fascinated by it, too, when the only fascination that existed within her was for him.

Luck made a move as if to stand, then paused. "Was there any coffee left?"

"Yes." She rose quickly to her feet. "I'll heat it up for you. It will only take a minute."

"I can get it." But Luck didn't protest too stridently, willing to let himself be persuaded to remain where he was.

"No, you stay here," Eve insisted. "I've been sitting so long I'm starting to get stiff. I need to move around a bit." Which was the truth, although the greater truth was a need to be alone and get herself together. She had to stop being torn apart by this unrequited love for him.

"Okay." Luck didn't argue the point further, remaining by the fire. "If you insist."

Activity helped as she buried herself in the kitchen, turning the coffee on to warm it through and setting out cups for each of them. Yet she couldn't forget that another woman had once brought him coffee and kissed his son good-night as she had done the previous evening. The latter thought prompted Eve to check on Toby while she waited for the coffee to heat.

When she entered the hallway, it was at the precise moment that Luck entered it from the living room. Eve stopped, a little guiltily.

"I thought I'd see if Toby was all right," she explained.

The slight curve to his mouth captivated her with its male charm. "That's where I was headed, too," Luck replied, lifting a dark brow in arching inquiry. "Shall we go together and both be satisfied?"

He took her agreement for granted, linking an arm around her waist to guide her down the darkened hallway. The sensation was much too enjoyable for Eve to resist. She was becoming satisfied with the crumbs of his attention— something she had believed her pride would never let her do.

The doorway to his room stood open and they paused in its frame, standing side by side. In the semidarkness they could see his shining face, all youthful innocence in sleep. His dark hair waved across his forehead like a cap. Deep affection for the sleeping child tugged at her heartstrings.

"That's about the only time he's quiet," Luck murmured softly.

A faint smile touched her mouth as Eve turned her head to look up at him in silent understanding. Toby was always doing, saying or up to something. She could well imagine the wry truth in Luck's comment.

When she met his downward glance, something warm and wonderful shone in his blue eyes. There was a caressing quality in the way they wandered over her upturned face. It started her heart pounding at a rapid speed.

He bent slightly toward her, brushing her lips in a light kiss that stirred her senses and left her wanting more. That desire trembled within her, not letting itself be known. Nothing invited it to show her wants, and Eve lacked the aggression and confidence to assert herself.

"Do you suppose the coffee's hot yet?" Luck murmured, not lifting his head very far from hers.

"It should be," she whispered, and doubted if her voice had the strength to speak louder.

As they turned to leave the doorway, neither of them noticed the little boy in bed cautiously open one eye, or the satisfied smile that smugly curved his mouth.

Luck accompanied her to the kitchen and carried his own cup of hot coffee into the living room. He walked past the sofa and chairs to the fireplace, lowering himself to sit on the floor in front of the dying fire. Reaching out, he pulled a couple of throw pillows from the sofa closer to his position and patted them to invite Eve to join him. She sat on one, bending her legs to the side and holding her cup in both hands.

"Toby likes you a lot, Eve," Luck remarked, eyeing her with a sidelong glance.

"I like him a lot, too," she admitted. "So I guess it's mutual."

"Toby and I have led a bachelor's life for a long time," he said, continuing to regard her steadily. "I always thought we managed very well." He paused for a brief second. "Tonight I realized there were a lot of things we've been missing. I'm glad you came to dinner this evening."

"I'm glad you asked me," Eve replied, and guessed at his loneliness.

His actions and words had proved that he liked her, that he even regarded her as reasonably attractive. She knew she should be happy about that, but there was a part of her that wished he could be insanely in love with her, wanting her above all other women. It was silly to wish for the moon when she had the glow of the firelight.

"What I'm trying to say is that meeting you has been one of the best things that has happened to us in a long while." Luck appeared determined to convince her of something, but Eve wasn't sure what it was.

She couldn't help noticing the way it was always "we" or "us," never "I" or "me." He was coupling himself with Toby. It was her effect on "them"—not "him." She lowered her gaze to the cup in her hands.

"I'm handling this badly, aren't I?" His voice held a sigh of self-amusement.

"I can't answer that because I don't know what you're trying to handle," Eve said, attempting to speak lightly but unable to look at him.

"It's really very simple." He curved a hand under her chin and turned it toward him. "I want to kiss you. I've been wanting to do it all evening, but I never found the opening. So I was trying to make one."

Her heart fluttered at the disturbing hint of desire in his blue eyes. Luck had finally said "I," and her senses were on a rampage, wild with the promise that the word held. With a total lack of concern for the deliberateness of his actions, he took the coffee cup from her hands and set it on the stone hearth beside his.

Her composure was so rattled that she wondered how Luck could go about this all so calmly. Anticipation had her trembling on the brink of raw longing for his embrace. The sensation was becoming so strong that Eve didn't think she could hide it.

When his hands closed on her arms to draw her to him, Eve abandoned herself to the emotional needs and wants searing within. The fire in the hearth was dying, but the one inside her was kindled to a full blaze by the sure possession of his hard male lips.

His hand burrowed into the thickness of her brown hair, holding its mass while he supported the back of her head as his driving kiss forced it backward. Her arms went around his middle, her sense of touch excited by the solidness of his muscled body, so hard and firm and virile.

A mist of sensuality swirled itself around her consciousness and made any thought of caution a hazy ill-defined one. His hand roamed along her spine, alternately caressing and urging her closer. Eve strained to comply and arched nearer. The unyielding wall of his body flattened her breasts, but it wasn't enough.

Her breathing was so shallow it was almost nonexistent when Luck dragged his mouth from her lips to nibble at her throat and trail its way up the pulsing vein to the sensitive hollow below her ear. Eve quivered with the intensity of the passions he was arousing.

"I've needed this for so long, Eve," he declared in a voice thick with desire, the heat of his breath inflaming her skin. "I've been so empty. Fill me up, Eve. Fill me up."

But she didn't need to be urged. Her hunger and emptiness had been as great as his. Her eagerly parted lips were already seeking his when his mouth came back to claim them. The whole weight of him was behind the kiss, bending her backward farther and farther until she slipped off the pillow onto the carpeted floor.

Within seconds they were lying together, and the hard pressure of his male body was making itself felt on every inch of hers. No longer needing to hold her, his hands were free to explore the soft curves that had been against him.

When Luck shifted his position to make a more thorough discovery, a shirt button caught in the eyelet lace of her blouse. He swore under his breath, impatient with the obstacle as Eve was. There was a reluctant delay as Luck paused to free the button. When his knuckles rubbed against a breast, Eve couldn't help breathing in sharply at the inadvertent contact, a white-hot rush of desire searing through her veins.

Her reaction didn't go unnoticed. The instant he had rid himself of the impediment, his hand covered her breast and a soft moan of satisfaction trembled from her throat. He kissed the source of the sound and unerringly found the pleasure point at the base of her neck that sent excited shivers over her skin.

With her eyes closed to lock the delirious sensations of supreme joy forever in her memory, Eve caressed the taut muscles of his shoulders. His deft fingers unfastened the front of her lace blouse and pushed the material aside. When his hand glided inside her brassiere and lifted a breast from its confining cup, she was a churning mass of desire.

Her clamoring needs were almost beyond endurance as his mouth traveled downward from her collarbone to nuzzle the slope of her breast. His leg was hooked across her thighs, and she was rawly conscious of his hard need outlined against her hip. The ache in her loins ran wild when his mouth circled the sensitive peak of her breast. She was writhing inside.

"I thought you told me only married people did that, dad."

CHAPTER EIGHT

TOBY'S VOICE shattered the erotic moment into a thousand pieces. Both of them froze at the sound of it. Then her fingers dug into his muscled arms in embarrassed panic when her suddenly widened eyes saw the pajama-clad boy leaning casually over the back of the couch.

Luck reacted swiftly, using his body as a shield to hide her nakedness while he quickly pulled her blouse over her breast. Eve had a glimpse of the savage anger that took over his hard features before he turned his head to glare at Toby.

"What the hell are you doing out of bed?" he demanded harshly.

"I woke up 'cause I was thirsty, so I came out to the kitchen to get a drink," his son explained, unabashed by the intimate scene he had interrupted and apparently oblivious to the awkward situation he was causing. "How come you were doing that if you and Eve aren't married?"

"You've got two seconds to get into your

bed," Luck warned. "Or, so help me, you won't be able to sit down for a month!"

"But I was only wondering—" Toby began to protest, frowning in bewilderment.

"Now!" Luck snapped the word and brought a knee up as if to rise and carry out his threat.

Toby pushed off the couch and started toward the hallway, grumbling to himself. "You keep telling me I should ask questions when I don't understand. I don't know why you're yelling at me for doing it."

"Go to your room and stay there." The line of his jaw was iron hard.

The response from Toby was a loud sigh that signaled compliance. The instant he was out of sight, Luck sat up and combed a hand through his hair before casting a grimly apologetic glance at Eve's reddened face. She sat up quickly, half turning from him to button her blouse, nearly mortified to death by the incident.

"I'm sorry, Eve," Luck sighed heavily.

"It wasn't your fault," she murmured self-consciously, and tried to restore some semblance of order to her tousled clothes.

She wasn't sure which embarrassed her more—what Toby had seen or what he might have seen if he'd come a few minutes later. She had been lost beyond control, her sense of morality completely abandoned.

"I'm going to have a talk with that boy." Irritation vibrated through his taut declaration.

"You shouldn't be angry with him." Despite the embarrassment Toby had caused, Eve defended his innocent role in the scene. She scrambled to her feet the minute she was decent, and Luck followed to stand beside her. She was too disconcerted by the incident to meet his eyes squarely, so her sidelong glance fell somewhere short of his face. "Toby didn't mean to do anything wrong."

"I wouldn't be too sure about that," Luck muttered, more to himself, as he sent a hard glance toward the hallway to the bedrooms.

Then he was bringing all of his attention back to her. She stiffened at the touch of his hand on her shoulder. There were still yearnings within her that hadn't been fully suppressed and she didn't want things to get out of hand twice.

"Eve—" he began in a low tone that seemed to echo the buried wants inside her.

She knew she didn't dare listen to what he wanted to say. "I think you'd better take me home, Luck," she interrupted him stiffly.

Even without looking at him, she sensed his hesitation and trembled inwardly at the thought of trying to resist him if he decided to persuade her to change her mind. She didn't think she'd have the strength of will for a long struggle.

"All right, I will." He gave in grudgingly and removed his hand from her shoulder.

"I think it's best," Eve insisted faintly.

"Of course." There was a clipped edge to his voice. "Give me a minute to tell Toby where I'm going."

"Yes," she murmured.

He moved reluctantly away from her and Eve shuddered uncontrollably when he was out of the room. She had known she loved him, but she hadn't guessed at the depth of that emotion. She had nearly lost all sense of morals for the sake of the moment. It was sobering to realize she would probably do it all over again, given the opportunity.

When Luck entered the bedroom, Toby looked at him with affronted dignity. The urge to grab the boy by the shoulders and shake him hard still rang strong within Luck. It was all he could do to hold onto his temper and not let it fly.

"I'm taking Eve home." The anger was there in his abrupt tone of voice. "When I get back, you and I are going to have a talk."

"Okay," Toby agreed with equal curtness. "But I don't see what you're so uptight about."

"Don't say another word," Luck warned. "Or we'll have that talk now."

Toby pressed his lips together in a thin straight line that showed his resentment for the browbeating tactics. Pivoting, Luck walked from the room.

His anger came from an unbridled instinct to protect Eve. It had run strong and hot within him, imposing the need to shelter her body with his own and later to lash out at his son for the mental harm he'd caused.

When he rejoined her in the living room, Luck noticed how much further she had withdrawn into her shell. His senses remembered the way she had responded to him without inhibition. They craved it again, but after the way his own son had embarrassed her, he couldn't bring himself to impose his desires on her to know again that wild feeling she had aroused.

Without a word she turned and walked to the door, avoiding his look. Left with no choice but to follow her, he turned his head to the side in a grim kind of despair. Powerful feelings began to make themselves known to him. Uppermost remained the need to right whatever damage had been done to her sensitive nature.

A RAW TENSION dominated the drive to her parents' lake cottage. Eve sat rigidly in the passenger seat, staring straight ahead. Luck had made a couple of attempts at conversation,

but her short one-word answers had ended it.
She felt that she didn't dare relax her guard for
a second or all her inner feelings would spew
forth.

She could only thank God she was adult
enough to recognize that Luck could want to
make love to her without being in love with her.
Her embarrassment would have been doubled
otherwise.

Luck stopped his car behind her father's
sedan. This time he switched off the engine and
got out to walk around the hood and open her
door. He silently accompanied her to the front
porch.

"Good night, Luck." Eve wanted to escape
inside the cabin without further ado, but he
wasn't of the same mind.

His hand caught her arm near the elbow.
"I'm not letting you go inside feeling the way
you do," he said.

"I'm all right," she lied.

His other hand cupped the side of her face, a
certain grimness in his expression. "I don't
want Toby's interference spoiling those moments for us."

"It doesn't matter." Eve tried to evade the
issue.

"It does matter," Luck insisted. "It matters a
great deal to me."

"Please." It was a protest of sorts against any
discussion of the subject.

His hand wouldn't let her move away from its touch. "I'm not ashamed of wanting to make love to you, Eve," he declared. "And I don't want you to be, either."

His bluntness seemed to weaken her knees. After avoiding his gaze for so long, she finally looked at him. His steady regard captured her glance and held it.

"Okay?" Luck wanted her agreement to his previous statement.

"Okay." She gave it in a whisper.

He kissed her warmly as if to seal the agreement, then lifted his head. "You and I will talk about this tomorrow," he said. "In the meantime, I've got to go back and have a little father-to-son chat with Toby."

"All right." Eve wasn't sure what he wanted to talk about, and that uncertainty was in her voice.

Luck heard it and seemed to hesitate before letting her go. "Good night, Eve."

"Good night." She called softly after him as he descended the porch steps to his car.

Returning to the cabin, Luck went directly to his son's bedroom. He switched on the light as he entered the room. Toby sat up and made a project out of arranging his pillows to lean against them. When Luck walked to the bed, Toby crossed his arms in a gesture that implied determined tolerance.

"Sit down, dad," he said. "I think it's time we talked this out."

Luck didn't find the usual amusement in his son's pseudoadult attitude and had to smother a fierce rush of irritation. "I'll sit down," he stated. "But I'm going to do the talking and you're going to listen."

"Whatever you say." Again there was an exhibition of patience with his father.

"Do you have any idea how much you embarrassed Eve?" Luck demanded, taking a position on the edge of the bed.

"You kinda lost your cool, too, dad," Toby pointed out calmly.

"I said I was going to do the talking," Luck reminded him sternly. "It wasn't so bad that you walked in when you did, Toby. The part that was wrong was when you stayed."

"I wanted to find out what was going on," he explained with wide-eyed innocence.

"It was none of your business," Luck countered. "There are certain times when a couple wants privacy."

"But you told me that happened when the two people were married." A faint light gleamed in Toby's eyes, betraying his supposed naiveté.

"That is beside the point." The line of his mouth became grim as Luck's gaze narrowed on his son. "Right now, I want you to understand that what you did was wrong and you owe Eve an apology.''

"Was what you and Eve were doing wrong?" Toby inquired.

"Toby." There was a warning in his father's voice not to sidetrack the conversation with his own questions.

"Okay," he sighed with mock exaggeration. "I'll apologize to Eve," Toby promised. "But since you like Eve and you want to do things with her that married people do, why don't you marry her? Did you find out if she has staples in her stomach?"

"Staples?" Luck frowned, briefly avoiding the first question.

"Don't you remember when we met that real sexy blonde on the beach and you said you didn't want to marry anyone with staples in her stomach?" Toby reminded him.

It took Luck a minute to recall his reference to the centerfold type. "No, Eve isn't the kind with staples," he replied.

"Then why don't you ask her to marry you?" Toby argued. "I'd really like it if she became my mother."

"You would, huh?" He tilted his head to one side in half challenge. "After what you pulled tonight, she might not be interested in becoming your mother even if I asked her."

A look of guilty regret entered Toby's expression. "She was really upset, huh?" He was worried by the question.

"Yes, she was. Thanks to you." Luck didn't lessen the blame.

"If I told her I was sorry, maybe then she'd say yes if you asked her," Toby suggested.

"I've already told you that you're going to apologize to her in the morning," he stated.

"Are you going to ask her to marry you after that?" Toby wanted to know.

"I don't recall even suggesting that I wanted to marry Eve," Luck replied.

"But you do, don't you?" Toby persisted.

"We'll talk about that another time." He avoided a direct answer. "Tonight you just think about what you're going to say to Eve tomorrow."

"Will you think about marrying her?" His son refused to let go of the subject as Luck straightened from the bed. Toby slid under the covers to lie down once again while Luck tucked him in.

"I'll think about it," he conceded.

"Good night, dad." There was a satisfied note in Toby's voice.

"Good night."

Luck was absently shaking his head as he walked from the room. After checking to make sure the fire in the fireplace was out, he went to his own room and walked to the dresser where Lisa's photograph stood. He picked it up and studied it for a minute.

"You know it isn't that I love you any less," he murmured to the picture. "What we had, I'll never lose. It's just that my love for Eve is stronger. You would have liked her."

He held the photograph for a minute longer, saying a kind of farewell to the past and its beautiful memories. With deep affection he placed the picture carefully inside one of the dresser drawers. He had not believed it possible to fall in love twice in a lifetime, but he had. Once as a young man—and now as a mature adult. By closing the drawer, he turned a page in his life.

A ROUND BEVERAGE TRAY was precariously balanced on Toby's small hand as he quietly turned the knob to open his father's door. The orange juice sloshed over the rim of its glass, but he miraculously managed not to spill the hot coffee. With both hands holding the tray once more, he walked to the bed where his father was soundly sleeping.

When he set the tray on the nightstand, Toby noticed something was missing. His mother's photograph was gone from the dresser. A smile slowly began to curve his mouth until he was grinning from ear to ear. He tried hard to wipe it away when he turned a twinkling look on his father.

"It's time to get up, dad." He shook a bronze shoulder to add action to his summons.

His father stirred reluctantly and opened a bleary eye. He closed it again when he saw Toby.

"Come on, dad." Toby nudged him again. "Wake up. It's seven-thirty. I brought you some orange juice and coffee."

This time both sleepy blue eyes opened and Luck pushed himself into a half-sitting position in the bed. Toby handed him the glass of orange juice and crawled onto the bed to sit cross-legged.

After downing the juice, Luck set the glass on the tray and reached for the pack of cigarettes and lighter on the nightstand.

"You are certainly bright-eyed this morning." There was a trace of envy in his father's sleep-thickened voice as he lit a cigarette and blew out a stream of blue gray smoke.

"I've been up awhile," Toby shrugged. "Long enough to make the coffee and have some cereal."

Luck picked up the coffee cup and took a sip from it. "After last night, I think it would be a good idea if you started knocking before walking into somebody's room."

"You mean, so I won't embarrass Eve when she starts sleeping in here after you're married," Toby guessed.

"Yes—" The affirmative reply was out before he realized what he'd admitted. The second he heard what he had said, he came instantly awake.

Toby laughed with glee. "You did decide to marry her!"

"Now, you wait just a minute," Luck ordered, but there wasn't any way he could retract his previous admission. "That doesn't mean Eve is willing to marry me."

"I know." Toby continued to grin widely. "You haven't asked her yet. When are you going to propose to her?"

"You will have to apologize for last night," Luck reminded him. "You aren't getting out of that."

"We can go over there this morning, just like we planned." Toby began laying out the strategy. "I'll apologize to her, then you can ask her to marry you."

"No, Toby." His father shook his head. "That isn't the way it's going to happen. We'll go over there and you'll apologize. That's it."

"Ahh, dad," Toby protested. "You're going to ask her anyway. Why not this morning?"

"Because you don't ask a woman to be your wife while there's an eight-year-old kid standing around listening," his father replied with mild exasperation.

"When are you going to ask her, then?" Toby demanded impatiently.

"I'm going to invite Eve to have dinner with me tonight," he said. "You're going to stay home and I'll have Mrs. Jackson come over to sit with you."

"Mrs. Jackson?" Toby cried with a grimace of dislike. "Why does she have to come over?"

"We've been through this before," Luck reminded him. "You aren't going to stay here by yourself."

"Well, why do you have to go out to dinner with Eve?" he argued. "Why can't she come over here like she did last night? I'll leave you two alone and promise not to listen."

His father sighed heavily and glanced toward the ceiling. "How can I make you understand?" he wondered aloud. "When a woman receives a marriage proposal, she has a right to expect a few romantic touches along with it—a little wine and candlelight. You don't have her come over, cook dinner, wash dishes, then propose. It just isn't done like that."

"It sure sounds like an awful lot of fuss to me," Toby grumbled. "Eve wouldn't mind if you just asked her without going through all that."

"I don't care whether she doesn't mind. I do," Luck stated, and crushed the half-smoked cigarette in the ashtray. "Off the bed," he ordered. "I want to get dressed."

"Are we going to Eve's now?" Toby hopped to the floor.

"Not this early in the morning," Luck told him. "We'll wait until later."

"But it's Sunday. She might go to church," he protested.

"Then we'll drive over there the first thing this afternoon."

"Aw, dad." Toby sighed his disappointment and left the bedroom dragging his feet.

IT WAS NOONTIME when Eve and her parents returned to the lake cottage from Sunday church services. Dinner was in the oven, so they were able to sit down to the table in short order. By one o'clock the dishes were done and Eve went to her room to change out of her good dress.

"Eve?" The questioning call from her mother was accompanied by a knock on the door. "Your father and I are going for a boat ride on the lake. Would you like to come with us?"

Zipping her jeans, Eve went to the door and opened it. "No, thanks, mom." She smiled at the woman with graying brown hair. "I think I'll just stay here and finish that book I was reading."

She didn't mention that Luck had indicated he would see her today. No definite arrangement had been made. Eve preferred that her parents didn't know that she was staying on the off chance he might come by or call.

"Is Eve coming with us?" her father asked from the front room.

"No," her mother answered him. "She's going to stay here."

"I'll bet she's expecting Luck McClure," he

declared on a teasing note, and Eve felt a faint blush warming her cheeks.

"Don't mind him," her mother declared with an understanding smile. "He's remembering the way I sat around the house waiting to hear from him when we were dating." She made a move to leave. "We probably won't be back until later this afternoon."

"Have a good time," Eve said.

"You, too," her mother called back with a wink.

CHAPTER NINE

TOBY WAS SLUMPED in the passenger seat of the car, a grimly dejected expression on his face. "Boy, I wish Mrs. Jackson had been busy tonight." He grumbled the complaint for the sixth time since Luck had phoned her to sit with him.

"She's coming and there's nothing you can do to change that," Luck stated, looking briefly away from the road at his son. "I don't want you pulling any of your shenanigans, either."

Toby was silent for a minute. "Have you thought about how expensive this is going to be, dad?" He tried another tactic. "You not only have to pay Mrs. Jackson to stay with me, but you've also got to pay for Eve's dinner and yours. With the money you're spending tonight, I'd have enough to buy my minibike. It sure would be a lot cheaper if you just asked her this afternoon."

"I don't want to hear any more about it." They had hardly been off the subject since this morning, and his patience was wearing thin.

"But don't I have some say in this?" Toby argued. "After all, she is going to be my mother."

"I wouldn't bring that up if I were you," Luck warned. "You haven't squared yourself with Eve about last night. She might not want to be the mother to a boy who doesn't respect other people's private moments."

"Yes, but I'm going to apologize for that," Toby reasoned. "Eve will understand. I'm just a little kid."

"Sometimes I wonder about that," Luck murmured to himself.

TAKING THE ICE-CUBE TRAY out of the freezer section of the refrigerator, Eve carried it to the sink and popped out a handful of cubes to put in the glass of tea sitting on the counter. The rest she dumped into a plastic container and set it in the freezer for later use. She turned on the cold water faucet to fill the ice-cube tray. The noise made by the running water drowned out the sound of the car pulling into the drive.

As she carried the tray full of water to the refrigerator, she heard car doors slamming outside. Her heart seemed to leap at the sound. In her excitement, Eve forgot about the tray in her hands and started to turn. Water spilled over the sides and onto the floor.

"Damn," she swore softly at her carelessness, and set the tray on the counter.

Hurriedly Eve tore some paper towels off the roll and bent down to sop up the mess. Her pulse raced with the sound of footsteps approaching the cottage. Her haste just seemed to make it take longer to wipe up the spilled water.

A knock rattled the screen door in its frame. She carried the water-soaked wad of paper towels to the sink, a hand cupped under them to catch any drips.

"I'm coming!" Eve called anxiously, and dropped the mess in the sink.

Her glance darted to the screen door and the familiar outline of Luck's build darkened by the wire mesh. She paused long enough to dry her hands on a terry towel and run smoothing fingers over her gleaming brown hair.

There was a wild run of pleasure through her veins as she hurried toward the door. Reflex action adjusted the knitted waistband of her carnation-red top around her snug-fitting jeans.

Eve didn't notice the shorter form standing next to Luck until she was nearly to the door, and realized he'd brought Toby with him. Not that she minded; it was just that Luck had indicated he wanted to talk to her privately. Toby's presence negated that opportunity. And there was the embarrassing matter of last night's scene. She was naturally modest, so there was a sense of discomfort in meeting Toby today.

"Hello." She greeted them through the screen and unlatched the door to open it. There was a nervous edge to her smile until she met the dancing warmth of Luck's blue eyes. It eased almost immediately as a little glow started to build strength. "Sorry it took so long, but I had to mop up some water I spilled."

"That's all right. We didn't wait that long," Luck assured her. The admiring run of his gaze over her face and figure seemed to give her confidence. She could tell he liked what he saw, even if she wasn't the type to turn heads.

"Hello, Toby." Eve was able to smile at the young boy without any strain as he entered the cottage at his father's side.

"Hi." His response seemed a little more subdued than normal, as if his mind were preoccupied with other matters, but his bright eyes were just as alert as they always were.

"Come in," Eve invited. "I just fixed myself a glass of iced tea. Would you two like some?"

Refusal formed on Luck's mouth, but Toby was quicker with his acceptance. "Yeah, I'd like a glass."

"And some cookies, too?" Eve guessed.

"Chocolate chip?" he asked hopefully, and she nodded affirmatively. "I sure would."

"What do you say?" Luck prompted his son to show some manners.

"Thank you," Toby inserted, then frowned. "Or was it supposed to be 'please'?"

"It doesn't matter," Eve assured him with a faint smile. "You've got the idea." Her glance lifted to the boy's father. "Did you want a glass of tea and some cookies?"

"I'll settle for the tea," he replied, changing his mind in the face of his son's acceptance.

The pair followed her into the small kitchen. Toby crowded close to the counter to watch her while Luck stayed out of her way, leaning a hip against a counter top and lighting a cigarette. Eve never lost her awareness of his lean masculinity, even though he wasn't in her line of vision. Her body's finely tuned radar was aware of his presence.

She fixed two more glasses of tea without any mishap and even managed to put the ice-cube tray filled with water in the refrigerator's freezer section without spilling any. Lifting the lid of the cookie jar, Eve took out three chocolate chip cookies and placed them on a paper napkin for Toby.

"Here you go, Toby." She turned to give them to him.

"Wait a minute," Luck stated, and laid a hand on his son's shoulder to stop him from taking them. "Before any refreshments are passed around, there's something Toby wants to say to you, Eve. Isn't there, Toby?" There was a prodding tone in his voice when he addressed his son.

A big sigh came from Toby as he lowered the

hand that had reached for the cookies. "Yes," he admitted, and turned his round blue gaze on Eve. "I'm sorry for embarrassing you last night. I didn't mean to."

"I know you didn't." She colored slightly at the reference to the incident.

"Dad explained about respecting other people's privacy," he said. "I was wrong to stay without you knowing I was there. I'm really and truly sorry, Eve. All I wanted to do was find out what was going on. I never meant to embarrass you."

Toby possessed more than his share of natural curiosity. She had known all along that he hadn't meant any harm. It was obvious he wasn't shocked by what he'd seen, which allowed her to feel that the scene between herself and Luck had been natural and right.

"It's all right, Toby," Eve promised him. "You're forgiven, so we can all forget about it."

His blue eyes widened in a hopeful look. "Then you aren't mad or upset about it?"

"No, not at all," she replied with a shake of her head.

Tipping his head back, Toby turned it to look up at his father. "See?" he challenged. "I told you she wouldn't be."

"I know you did," Luck admitted. "But she deserved an apology just the same."

"Now will you ask her to marry you instead

of—" Toby didn't get the question finished before Luck clamped a hand over his mouth to muffle the rest of it.

An electric shock went through Eve as her gaze flew to Luck's face. Her own complexion had gone pale at Toby's suggestion. His ruggedly virile features held grim impatience and displeasure in their expression, and Eve knew she had been right to doubt that Toby knew what he was talking about. It seemed she had been catapulted from one awkward situation into another.

"Toby, I could throttle you," Luck muttered angrily, and took his hand from the boy's mouth. "Don't you dare say another word."

"But—" Toby frowned his lack of understanding.

"I mean it," Luck cut across his voice with stern reproval. "Get your cookies and iced tea and go outside," he ordered. "I don't want to hear so much as a peep out of you."

"Okay," Toby grumbled, and moved to the counter to take the napkin of cookies and a glass of iced tea. Eve was too frozen to help him.

"You stay outside and don't come walking back in," Luck warned. "Remember what you promised me about that."

"Yes, dad," he nodded, and trudged toward the screen door.

Eve continued to stare at Luck as he snubbed

the cigarette butt in an ashtray on the counter. There was regret in the hard line of his mouth and a grim apology in his eyes when he finally looked at her. She heard the door bang shut behind the departing Toby.

"I'm afraid my son has a big mouth," Luck said.

A terrible pain wrenched at her heart. She turned away to hide it, clasping the edge of the counter with both hands. Dredging deep into the well of her reserve strength, she found a little piece of composure.

"Don't worry about it," Eve declared with forced lightness. "I'm not going to hold you to Toby's suggestion, so no marriage proposal is expected."

Her pulse raced as Luck moved to stand behind her. His hands settled lightly on the rounded points of her shoulders. At the moment she wasn't up to resisting his touch. A tremor of longing quivered through her senses.

"Why not?" he murmured, very close to her.

She pretended not to understand. "Why not what?" Her voice wavered.

"Since Toby has already let the cat out of the bag, I might as well ask you to marry me now, instead of waiting," Luck replied.

She half turned to look at him over her shoulder. He couldn't possibly be serious, but his steady gaze seemed to imply that he was. She was afraid to believe it. She loved him so much that it didn't seem possible her wildest dream might come true.

"Luck, you don't have to do this." She gave him a chance to retract his semiproposal.

That lazy half smile lifted a corner of his mouth, potent in its male charm. "I know I don't," he agreed.

"Then...." Eve continued to hesitate.

"I want you to be my wife," Luck said in an effort to make it clear to her that he was serious. It wasn't any kind of cruel joke. "And Toby wants you to be his mother—although I wouldn't blame you if you have second thoughts about taking on that role. He talks when he shouldn't— he sees things he shouldn't—and he knows things he shouldn't. It isn't going to be any bed of roses."

"I don't mind." She breathed the reply because she was beginning to believe that he meant all this.

"You'd better be sure about that." He turned her around to face him and let his hands slide down her back to gather her closer to him. "We haven't known each other long. I don't want to rush you into something. If you want to think it over, I'll wait for your answer."

Spreading her hands across the front of his shirt, Eve could feel his body warmth through the material. The steady beat of his heart assured her that this was all real. It wasn't a dream.

"It isn't that." Eve hadn't realized that she hadn't got around to accepting his proposal until that minute. "I'd like to marry you."

Luck tipped his head toward her. "Did I hear a but at the end of that?" he questioned.

"No." She hadn't said it, not in so many words; yet it was there—silently. "It's just so sudden. I can't think why you'd want to marry me," she admitted at last.

"I want to marry you for the usual reason." A warm dryness rustled his voice. "I love you, Eve."

The breath she drew in became lodged in her throat. She hadn't realized what beautiful words they were until Luck uttered them. An incredulous joy misted her eyes.

"I love you, too," she declared in a voice choked with emotion.

His mouth closed on hers and there was no more need for words. Her hands slid around his neck and into the thickness of his dark hair as his molding arms crushed her to his length. Eve reeled under the hard possession of his kiss, still dazed that he actually wanted her. But he seemed determined to prove it with action as well as words.

When her parted lips were at last convinced, Luck showered her face with rough kisses. Her eyes, her brows, her cheeks, her nose, her chin, her jaw—no part of her was exempted from his hungry foray. It left her so weak she could hardly breathe. Her racing heart threatened to burst from the love swelling within her.

The searing pleasure of it all was a sweet ache that throbbed through her limbs. His hands leisurely roamed her shoulders, back and hips to caress and arouse her flesh to a fever pitch of delight. For Eve there was no holding back. She gave him her heart and soul in return, and anything else he wanted—her pride, her dignity, her self-respect. It was all his.

A faint tremor went through him when Luck lifted his head an inch or so from hers to study her with a heavy-lidded look of desire. "I thought it would take more convincing than this to persuade you to marry me," he admitted huskily.

"Hardly." Eve smiled at that, knowing she had been his for the taking a long time now.

He withdrew a hand from her back to cup her upturned face. She turned into its largeness and pressed a kiss in its palm. His fingers began a tactile examination of her features from the curve of her cheekbone to the outline of her lips.

"That night I bumped into you outside the tavern, I knew I didn't want to let you go," Luck murmured. "But I didn't dream that I'd eventually marry you."

Even though their first meeting was a special and vivid memory, Eve wished he hadn't mentioned it. She didn't want to remember that he had regarded her as a brown mouse. She closed her eyes to shut it out.

"I thought you were a figment of my imagination," he went on, and slid his hand to her neck, where his thumb stroked the curve of her throat. "Until I finally recognized you that rainy afternoon you came to help Toby bake cookies. And there you were, right in my own home."

"I remember," Eve admitted softly, but she wasn't enthused about the subject.

Luck drank in a deep breath and let it out slowly. "Before I met you, I was beginning to think I wasn't capable of caring for another woman."

There was an instantaneous image in her mind of the photograph of his first wife. A painful sweep of jealousy washed over her because she would never be first in his life. She loved him so much that she was willing to settle for being second as long as it meant she could spend her life with him.

"Toby has been wanting me to get married for some time," Luck told her. "He even chose you before I did. I have to admit my son has very good taste."

Eve smiled faintly. "He's still outside—and probably dying of curiosity."

"Let him." His arm tightened fractionally around her waist. "It's what he deserves." Then Luck sighed reluctantly. "I suppose we should let him in on the news, although he was positive you'd agree to marry me.''

"He was right." She basked in the blue light of his unswerving gaze.

"He's never going to let us hear the end of it. You know that, don't you?" he mocked lightly.

"Probably not," Eve agreed with a widening smile.

"We might as well go tell him," Luck finally agreed with her suggestion.

As he turned to guide her out of the kitchen, he kept his arm curved tightly around her and her body pressed close to his side. It was a very possessive gesture and it thrilled Eve.

When they walked outside, they found Toby sitting on the porch steps waiting patiently—or perhaps impatiently, judging by how quickly he bounded to his feet to greet them. His bright glance darted eagerly from one to the other.

"Did she say yes?" he asked Luck with bated breath.

"What makes you think I asked her?" Luck challenged.

He cast an anxious look at Eve, who was trying not to smile. "You did, didn't you?" Again the question was addressed to his father.

"I did." Luck didn't keep him in the dark any longer. "And Eve agreed to be my wife."

"Whoopee!" Toby shouted with glee and practically jumped in the air. "I knew she would," he rubbed it in to his father. "I told

WITH A LITTLE LUCK

you that you didn't have to wait until tonight, didn't I?''

Luck glanced at Eve to explain. ''I was going to do it up right. I had it all planned—to take you out to dinner, ply you with champagne, sway you with candlelight and flowers. Then I was going to propose. Unfortunately, blabber-mouth jumped the gun.''

''Now you don't have to do that,'' Toby inserted. ''And I don't have to stay with Mrs. Jackson. Eve can come over to our place tonight and we'll all have dinner together.''

''No, she can't,'' Luck stated, shaking his head.

Toby frowned. ''Why can't she come?''

''Because I'm taking her out to dinner just the way I planned,'' he said. ''And Mrs. Jackson is coming over to stay with you just as we arranged it.''

''Dad,'' he protested.

''I'm going to have to share her with you a lot of evenings in the future, but on the first night of our engagement, I'm going to have her all to myself,'' Luck declared.

''I'd stay in my room,'' Toby promised.

''That isn't the same,'' he insisted, and looked again at Eve. ''You will have dinner with me tonight if I promise you you won't have to cook it?''

''Yes.'' Even if she had to cook it, she would have agreed.

"I'll come over early, around seven, so I can talk to your parents." Luck smiled as he realized, "I haven't asked you how soon you'd like the wedding to be?"

His phrasing of the question—not "when" but "how soon"—nearly took her breath away. For a second she could only look at him, a wealth of love shining in her eyes.

"The sooner the better, don't you think?" she suggested, a little tentatively.

"Absolutely." His answer was very definite as he bent his head to claim her lips once more.

What started out as a brief kiss lingered into something longer. Eve leaned more heavily against him, letting his strength support her. Before passion could flare, they were reminded that they weren't alone.

"I have a question," Toby said, interrupting their embrace.

"What is it?" But Luck was more than a little preoccupied with his study of her soft lips.

"Am I supposed to leave you two alone every time you start kissing?" he asked.

"Not necessarily every time. Why?" Luck dragged his gaze from her face to glance curiously at his son.

"If I did, it just seems to me that I might be spending an awful lot of time by myself," Toby sighed. "And I'd really kinda hoped the three of us could be together like a family."

"We *will* be a family," Eve assured him. "And you won't be spending much time alone."

"Eve's right." Luck reached out to curve an arm around his son's shoulders and draw him into their circle. "Part of the plan was for you to have a mother, wasn't it?"

"Yep." Toby smiled widely.

CHAPTER TEN

THE THREE OF THEM spent the afternoon together, partly to allay Toby's concern about his position in the new family unit and partly because Luck and Eve enjoyed Toby's company and shared a mutual desire to include him. Eve knew she was just imagining it, but the sun seemed to shine brighter and the air smelled fresher than it ever had before.

Her parents hadn't returned from their boat ride by the time Luck and Toby left to go home. Eve had some time alone to think over the unexpected proposal and all that had been said. She finally came out of the wonderful daze that had numbed her to a few home truths.

Luck had asked her to marry him for many reasons. He had said that he loved her, and she didn't doubt that in his own way he did. But she realized he didn't love her as much as she loved him. Another factor was Toby: he had needed and wanted a mother, and he had liked her. He'd undoubtedly had a lot of influence on Luck's decision. That was only natural.

Plus Eve had known he was a lonely man. He

wanted the company of a woman—and not just in a sexual way, for she was sure he could find that type of feminine company. That night in front of the tavern, Luck had said he wanted to talk to her—that she was the kind he could talk to. He needed that in a woman, just as she needed to be able to talk to him. But part of his reason for proposing had to be the desire for companionship.

Then there was the bachelor existence he and Toby led. They needed someone to cook and clean house for them. How much more convenient it would be to have live-in help. Cooking and cleaning would be part of her new role, although naturally both Luck and Toby would help.

There was nothing wrong with any of his reasons. None of them were bad. As a matter of fact there were a lot of couples starting out their wedded life with less solid foundations than theirs. But the realizations brought Eve down out of her dreamworld to face the reality of their future. Luck wanted to marry a comfortable, practical Eve, not a starry-eyed romantic. It was better that she knew that.

It didn't alter the special significance of the evening to come. It was still their engagement dinner. Eve took extra care in choosing a dress to wear and fixing her hair and makeup. The results weren't too bad, even to her critical eye. The rose color of the dress was a little drab, but its lines flattered her slender figure. The soft curls of her chestnut hair glistened in the light.

True to his word, Luck arrived promptly at seven, with a bouquet of scarlet roses for Eve. She hadn't mentioned anything to her parents about his proposal, waiting until he came so they could tell them together.

They were overjoyed at the news, especially her mother, who had despaired that Eve would ever find a man to satisfy her. Her father seemed to take pride in Luck's old-fashioned gesture of asking his permission to marry his daughter. It was granted without any hesitation.

By half-past seven the congratulations were over and they were on their way to the restaurant. Eve realized how difficult it was to keep both feet on the ground when she was with Luck. Her hand rested on the car seat, held in the warm clasp of his.

"Are you happy?" he asked.

"Yes." She could say that without any doubt, even with the facts before her concerning his reasons for wanting to marry her.

"I thought we could drive to Duluth tomorrow," he said. "I need to buy you a ring, but I want to be sure you like it. We'll pick something out together. Is tomorrow all right?"

"Yes, it's fine," Eve nodded.

"I want you to meet my father while we're there. We'll have dinner with him," he stated.

"That would be good," she agreed. "I'd like to get to know him."

"You'll like him." He sent her a brief smile. "And I have no doubt that he'll like you."

"I hope so." But she was secretly concerned that his father would compare her with Luck's first wife and wonder what his son saw in such a "plain Jane." A lot of his friends who had known his first wife would probably wonder about that, also. She wouldn't blame them if they did.

"Would you mind if Toby came with us tomorrow?" Luck asked as he slowed the car to turn into the restaurant parking lot.

"Of course I don't mind," Eve assured him. "If we don't include him, he'll probably become convinced he's being neglected."

"That's what I thought, too," he agreed, and parked the car between two others.

After climbing out of the car, Luck walked around it to open her door and help her out. He lingered on the spot, holding her hand and smiling at her.

"Have I told you that you look very lovely tonight?" he asked.

"No, but thank you." Eve smiled, but she wondered if he was just being kind. Perhaps it was a nice way of saying she looked as good as she could look.

Bending his head, he let his mouth move warmly over hers. The firm kiss didn't last long, but it reassured her of his affection. Eve doubted if that brief kiss disturbed him as much as it disturbed her, though.

When it was over, he escorted her to the restaurant entrance, his hand pressed against the back of her waist. Inside they were shown to a small table for two in a quiet corner of the establishment.

"Didn't I promise you candlelight?" Luck gestured to the candle burning in an amber glass when they were both seated in their chairs across from each other.

"Yes, you did," she agreed with a remembering smile. "You neglected to mention the soft music playing in the background." Eve referred to the muted strains of romantic mood music coming over the restaurant's stereo system.

"I saved that for the finishing touch." The corners of his mouth deepened in a vague amusement.

A young and very attractive waitress approached their table. With her blond hair and blue eyes, she seemed the epitome of everything sexy, without appearing vulgarly so. She smiled at both of them, yet Eve jealously thought she noticed something other than professional interest in the girl's eyes when she looked at Luck.

"Would you like a drink before dinner?" she inquired.

"Yes, we'd like a bottle of champagne," Luck ordered with a responding smile.

Eve would probably have checked his pulse to see if he was sick if he hadn't noticed the blonde's obvious beauty. Yet when he did she was hurt. It made no sense at all. Somehow she managed to keep the conflicting emotions out of her expression.

The waitress left and came back with the bottle of champagne. After she had opened it, she poured some in a glass for Luck to sample. He nodded his approval and she filled a glass for each of them.

When she'd gone, Luck raised his glass to make a toast. "To the love of my life, who is soon to be my wife."

It was a very touching sentiment, but Eve knew it was an exaggeration. He had promised her a romantic evening and he was trying to give it to her, but she would rather their relationship remained honest and did not become sullied with false compliments.

"That was very beautiful, Luck," she admitted. "But it wasn't necessary."

"Oh?" His eyebrow arched at her comment. "Why isn't it necessary?"

"Because—" she shrugged a shoulder a little nervously "—I didn't expect you to pretend that you are wildly and romantically in love with me. You don't have to make flowery speeches."

"I see." The line of his jaw became hard, even though he smiled. "And it doesn't bother you if I'm not wildly and romantically in love with you?'' There was a trace of challenge in his question.

Eve assured him, ''I've accepted it.'' She didn't want him to act the part of a romantic lover when it wasn't what he truly felt.

''I'm glad you have,'' he murmured dryly, and motioned for the waitress to bring them menus. ''I understand the prime rib is very good here.''

The dinner conversation was dominated by mundane topics. The meal was very enjoyable, yet Eve sensed some underlying tension. Luck was pleasant and friendly, but sometimes when he looked at her she felt uneasy. He'd always been able to disturb her physically, yet this was different—almost as if he were angry, though he didn't appear to be.

The dinner had stretched to a second cup of coffee after dessert before Luck suggested it was time to leave. Eve accepted his decision, still unable to put her finger on the source of the troubling sensation.

In silence they crossed the parking lot to the car. Luck assisted her into the passenger seat, then walked behind the car to slide into the driver's seat. He made no attempt to start the car.

''Is something wrong?'' Eve frowned slightly.

''There seems to be,'' he said with a nod, and half turned in the seat to face her.

''What is it?'' She wasn't sure if he meant